**THE LONGEST WAY TO EAT A MELON**

# THE LONGEST WAY TO EAT A MELON

JACQUELYN ZONG-LI ROSS

SARABANDE BOOKS
LOUISVILLE, KENTUCKY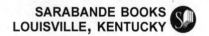

Copyright © 2025 Jacquelyn Zong-Li Ross
FIRST EDITION
All rights reserved.
No part of this book may be reproduced without written permission of the publisher.

Publisher's Cataloging-In-Publication Data
(Provided by Cassidy Cataloguing Services, Inc.).

Names: Ross, Jacquelyn (Editor), author.
Title: The longest way to eat a melon / Jacquelyn Zong-Li Ross.
Description: First edition. | Louisville, Kentucky : Sarabande Books, [2025]
Identifiers: ISBN: 9781956046410 (paperback) | 9781956046427 (ebook)
Subjects: LCSH: Creative ability—Fiction. | Self—Fiction. | Twins—Fiction. | Artists—Fiction. | Brain—Fiction. | Self-doubt—Fiction. | Absurd (Philosophy)—Fiction. | LCGFT: Short stories.
Classification: LCC: PS3618.O8452647 L66 2025 | DCC: 813.6—dc23

Cover design by Emily Mahon.
Interior design by Meg Reid.

Cover artwork is "Kittens and snail" by Alfred Brunel de Neuville (1852-1941) via Christie's Images / Bridgeman Images.
Excerpt from *Dunce* by Mary Ruefle. Copyright © 2020. Reprinted by permission of Wave Books. All Rights Reserved.
Excerpt from *DEBRIEFING: Collected Stories* by Susan Sontag, edited by Benjamin Taylor. Copyright © 2017 by David Rieff. Reprinted by permission of Farrar, Straus and Giroux. All Rights Reserved.

Printed in USA.
This book is printed on acid-free paper.
Sarabande Books is a nonprofit literary organization.

This project is supported in part by an award from the National Endowment for the Arts. The Kentucky Arts Council, the state arts agency, supports Sarabande Books with state tax dollars and federal funding from the National Endowment for the Arts.

We know more than we can use. Look at all this stuff
I've got in my head: rockets and Venetian churches,
David Bowie and Diderot, nuoc mam and Big Macs,
sunglasses and orgasms.

—Susan Sontag, "Debriefing"

From this day forward all plants
except the ~~lemon~~ *melon* tree
will be banished from my poems

—Mary Ruefle, "Vow of Extinction"

**CONTENTS**

| | |
|---|---|
| 1 | A Woman Suffering |
| 19 | Twenty-Three Versions of Disaster |
| 23 | Dreaming Against Capitalism |
| 35 | A Journey, Some Riches, Some Castles, Some Garbage |
| 41 | A Brief History of Feeling |
| 49 | Tiger Balm |
| 65 | Autobiography of a Lover |
| 73 | Opinion Generator |
| 75 | Elementary Brioche |
| 111 | Twelve Forecasts |
| 117 | Brain, No Brain |
| 131 | The Longest Way to Eat a Melon |
| 139 | The Breath of Han & Han |
| | Notes |
| | Acknowledgments |

## A WOMAN SUFFERING

She introduced herself as A Woman Suffering from a Crisis of Faith. By all accounts, Crisis of Faith led a pretty normal life—eating California Veggie Burgers (without the bun) at least once a week, working a not-too-bad four-day-a-week gig at the gallery gift shop, and thrifting for linen dresses when it was important to get outside. Except that in everything she did, she was unhappy. She'd once tried for a matter of weeks to dissolve the feeling by natural and pharmaceutical means, but her efforts, and their lack of results, only left her feeling more distraught. She'd lie in bed, chain-smoking, in her beige underwear until noon, at a complete loss for how to describe her suffering. She'd once tried to call it "gloominess" or "melancholia," but felt these failed to properly account for the emotional frenzy of her days; "in emotional distress" on the other hand seemed too clinical and dismissive, leaving out some vital social dimension. "Delirious" did nothing but place her in a fever state, "despondent" made it sound like she was hopeless or a coward, and "hysterical," with its etymological roots in a female nervous disorder "of the womb," was straight-out rejected by her feminism. When she finally settled on "crisis of faith" then, she did so not merely because she'd once believed but no longer believed in God, but because it most closely approximated the emphatic disillusionment she felt—with herself, and with the world. She felt immediately glad when she settled on what to call it.

She eventually quit her job and flew to the jungle where she would come to blame an unfortunate sequence of people, animals, and events for failing to deliver her spiritual awakening.

Enter Crisis of Faith, arguing loudly with some people in a field:

"What do you mean I can't take her with me?" She was crying, gesturing erratically at the stray dog she'd found outside the hacienda. The locals insisted she was diseased: that she had tapeworms and hookworms and whipworms, etcetera. One of the local boys whom she by now considered a friend shrugged sympathetically. She'd only known him three weeks, and just yesterday he'd led her up an unmarked trail to a secret parrots' cave at the edge of a waterfall, insisting that no healing would ever be found at the larger, more touristy cave located farther down the slope. He was just sixteen, a patch of stubble sprouting haphazardly from the ball of his chin, the hair on his head squeaky-clean and smelling of Pantene Pro-V. He was probably falling in love with her, she thought, without even meaning to think it, and it would probably be devastating. Already it seemed he knew a few things about spiritual journeys.

Fleas jumped off the dog's sandy rump from a patch of hair that was shorter than the rest, and the dog had such gentle eyes, so wide and brown, that when she looked straight into them she felt as if she might fall in. She'd had a dog just like it as a child and, deep down inside, maybe even in her actual heart, she felt that *this* dog was *that* dog, that *that* dog hadn't just died like everyone had told her it had, and here it was, still waiting for her companionship.

She told the dog to sit, and, when it refused, she gave it a kiss and a scratch behind the ears anyway. Then she told the dog to stay and ran off through the vacant lot to the store on the corner to buy a fine leash and fine collar, the finest in all the world, plus a dog bone, a dog bed, and a fine chew toy. When she returned a few minutes later, however, the dog was gone. This came as a surprise to no one but her.

Crisis of Faith would never see the dog again. But more importantly, this pattern of finding, then losing, the thing that might have brought her great happiness continued to be a philosophically troubling problem for her. Of *course* she blamed herself. She wondered about her suitability as a friend, as a caregiver, as a companion, about her ability to love and be loved in return. Logically, you might wonder whether Crisis of Faith had ever had a lover—a lover Crisis of Faith had never had.


Saturn returns every twenty-nine and a half years to the exact place in the sky where it was when a person was born. It is said that with it comes a period of heartbreak, financial ruin, existential crisis, the first onset of chronic pain, religious cults, tranquilizers, career setbacks, impulsive haircuts and tattoos—in short, the crash and burn of one's entire life, ideally followed by the birth of a phoenix from the ashes.

Crisis of Faith was precisely twenty-nine and a half years old when she boarded that plane to Mesoamerica, a coincidence that was not lost on her. In fact, she'd been anticipating the date of her Saturn return for some time, hoping that, given her already permanent state of crisis, the spontaneous purchase of a one-way ticket to the healing caves of Los Aullidos, named #1 Most Enchanting Destination by *Travel + Leisure* just this year or last, would bring about a transformation of exactly the opposite kind: complete and utter calm, creativity, clarity.

She'd decided that she was going to make a great adventure of it, despite being, at best, a sheltered type, a homely type, a type with eccentric indoor interests. She was very good, for example, at scrapbooking and oversized puzzles, and more recently had even become quite skilled in the art of decorative tile painting and mosaic, producing a surprising array of designs with the limited paint colors and tiles provided by the standard kits.

But the transformation didn't occur on the tarmac, as she'd hoped. Nor did it happen when she arrived at her destination some six and a half hours later, nor when she was finally delivered by cab to the doorstep of her hotel many hours after that. Day piled onto night onto day until her relentless self-pity became almost boring in its incessant climaxing. "What will become of me *now*…and *now*…and *now*?" she cried into her thrice-a-day cold-water shower as her discordant sobs blended effortlessly with the mournful song of at least six species of rare bird. She paced the windowed length of the tiny room she'd booked at the hacienda in the center of town (chosen not for its view, but its banana-leaved bar) and ordered redundant tequila sunrises and bowls and bowls of guacamole and chips, charged to American Express, just to temper her own disenchantment. She started early—think: *sunrise on sunrise*—to make room for the debilitating headache that she knew would seize her by three. And since, when her headache finally receded, it would be dark, and much too dark, she was told, for a foreigner to go wandering, she spent evenings in her hotel room reading deeply and melancholically from several canonical books of travel writing that she hoped might offer some clue as to the *right* way of bringing about the kind of sensual, process-driven, site-specific epiphany she was after. From D. H. Lawrence's *Mornings in Mexico*: "There is a little smell of carnations...a resinous smell of ocote wood...a smell of coffee...and perspiration and sun-burned earth and urine." How was she to smell *anything* in this place, she thought aloud, atop the nauseating poverty and richness of *so much feeling*?

Her internet-browser history, meanwhile, was a slough of distraught search queries mixed in with other troubling engine-generated ones: "woman + ruin," "how to ruin a woman emotionally," "how to destroy a man in bed," "how feminism ruined my life." She was persuaded by the various spiritual teachers she followed online to order Bibles and assorted self-help DVDs (none of which ever arrived, thanks to a single mistaken digit in the hotel postal code), and bought armfuls of colorful folk art gourds, placing them cheerfully around her hotel room like talismans. On good days, she set out boldly down the street in her best linen dress, ordering esquites on the corner just like the good travel book told her to, only to scrunch up her face and abandon the Styrofoam cup on the curb.

Still, she carried a rustic notebook around with her everywhere, and took very seriously the project of jotting down her musings about this, that, and whatever. *Authenticity is in the details*, she reminded herself, taking note of the peculiar fold of her skirt beneath the peculiar coral-colored drapery; the peculiar quality of the light in the hotel courtyard; the peculiar surrealist minotaur sculpture raging at the center of the garden, the peculiar angle of its penis, its balls, its thighs; and the clouds, their weird, anthropomorphic shapes...all these real-world models of how to live, by which she meant: without answers, yet also without crisis.

The first time she met Folk Art he was at a tiny roadside stand, drinking a minibottle of Coca-Cola and selling terra-cotta bowls in the shade. The first thing he said to her was that the zipper of her purse was open, and Crisis of Faith was so touched by the stranger's concern that she found herself lingering by the man's stall, fingering all his bowls, and wondering if he might be falling in love with her. She observed the young man furtively out of the corner of one eye as he crossed and uncrossed his legs from his seat on a blue plastic cooler behind the table. She picked up a teal-colored bowl with little pink dogs dancing all over it and ran her sweaty finger around the rim. It had been some time since she'd chatted in earnest with someone. She asked him whether the paints he used were food safe.

"My domain is purely aesthetic," he said, placing his right hand over his heart, leaning forward with a winning smile. "I am but a humble messenger of beauty."

Crisis of Faith looked him up and down, not knowing quite what to make of his response. It seemed to her impossible to tell, in that instant, whether he was going for some kind of *effect*, you know, or whether he'd just picked up English by accident once while dabbling in nineteenth-century classics. In the end, she felt she had no choice but to trust that this person would be unlikely to poison her—at least, not intentionally. The man had on a pair of navy slacks and a button-up linen shirt with bright-blue stitching, both neatly ironed, showing off their fresh creases. He had an open face, full and kind, and wholesome dimples that appeared when he smiled.

"Beauty," he said again. "All the dogs on there are portraits of my missing dog, Beauty. She was such a good dog," he said mournfully, before pointing again to the bowl. "Three hundred pesos," he said. "How about it?"

She held the bowl up to the light and felt that familiar rush of touristic vanity. *Yes*, she thought, *I must have it*, feeling very sure that this object would bring about the end of her suffering.

She rummaged around in her purse for her wallet, but found it missing just as Folk Art had foreseen. Why was she sweating so much? She was always sweating.

"I'm sorry, my wallet must be back at the hotel…"

Folk Art shrugged sympathetically and returned to a text message he was composing on a phone in his lap.

"But it's at least forty minutes to my hotel and back again," she continued, "and pretty soon it'll be dark. Could we call it an IOU?"

Folk Art chuckled but did not look up.

"It will be gone by tomorrow, I'm sure of it," she added.

"Miss, who do you take me for?" an impatient Folk Art finally replied. "Either you pay or don't pay, but I don't want any trouble…"

Some of the neighboring vendors stopped what they were doing to smile and watch whatever was unfolding. Crisis of Faith flushed with embarrassment. She could feel the prickle of a heat rash developing in the narrow crevice between her breasts. She puffed up her chest and tried not to scratch.

"You must think I'm just another silly foreigner, right? Another silly girl without a clue, wandering the world, cluelessly? You think I don't have a clue!" They laughed. "Well, what if I told you that I am also an *artist*? What if I told you that, just as you do, I spend much of my day thinking about how to form my small life into a life of *great beauty*?"

The other vendors swelled with laughter now, with no further effort made to disguise their pleasure. This made Crisis of Faith really angry. She felt tears backing up in her eyes, her ears, her throat. Eventually, there was nowhere left for them to go but out.

"Not everyone in America eats McDonald's, you know!" she spewed. "And don't go thinking everyone is a fucking evangelist either!"

How exhausting it was to be in a permanent state of crisis!

"I mean, if given the *opportunity* as a child I might have *loved* to—"

Folk Art squinted at her, hard. A disjointed expression came over his face then, like he was trying to solve a ten-thousand-piece puzzle. He stood up and put his Coke down on the lid of the cooler.

"Miss, are you...okay?"

"...Am I what?"

Folk Art flicked his fingers against his cheeks and pointed to her. She put her own hand to her cheek and agreed it felt warm.

"Oh. I'm fine," she said, as hot shapes lapped against her eyeballs.

How silly she must look to others! How fragile and girlish! How naive! Her body shuddered and filled with terror. She grabbed hold of the corner of the table for support as her knees, the very ground, shook below her. Strange timing for an earthquake, she remembered thinking, when all she'd ever wanted to be was in all aspects stable. Reliable, happy, funny, fun. All she wanted was to be loved. She wanted, even, to be liked.

She looked at Folk Art and tried to imagine that he was not a stranger at all, but someone she had known, and loved, and someone who had loved her back, and then she worked on projecting this imagined-love kind of feeling from the past into the present and into the future just to have something to move her beyond her fear of further unraveling. She looked at his face as the heat bent it into a big, vibrating dome, and found herself considering how she might go about falling in love with a person for the first time—strategically, but also, in a real way—how she might fall in love with a person, like, for example, him—and what that might feel like, to make herself even more vulnerable than she already was. Would it feel good? Would it feel terrible? The image of him before her went all wavy and limp.

The concerned look on Folk Art's face deepened and it confused her. *What are you so afraid of?* she thought. *What's the worst thing that could possibly happen?* She looked at the sky—its purity, its optimism, its obscenity—and watched it crash cinematically into the horizon.


Enter Crisis of Faith, despairing loudly at the top of a volcano, at the bottom of a sandy pit, or else at the edge of a rare kind of waterfall that only appears once a year during the rainy season:

"If I cannot *unbecome* my suffering, what will it take to make me a better suffering woman? A more charismatic woman? A more attractive crisis of faith?"

The sky was streaked the most vibrant purple; everyone she'd ever known bobbing around her, their floating, oversized heads and hands all rainbow-colored and psychedelic, their lips moving all at the same time so it was impossible to make out any of it, their wisdom. She'd apparently just been out running because she was dripping. She'd run somewhere just to stand there and yell, without caring much about finding her way back.

She imagined the mountain, or the bottom of the pit, or the cliff face breaking open and showering her with something like graduation glitter. She imagined her body breaking open and a new body stepping out. *Here at last: woman, faith.* Now what would it take?

She came to with a cooler of ice over the head.

"Stop it!" she screamed. "I said stop that immediately!"

Folk Art put the cooler back down on the ground and sat on it, wiping the sweat from his eyebrow hairs. "Take it easy," he said. "You passed out."

She touched her trembling hand to her temple and saw that she was bleeding.

"But now that you're back," he said, "you can help me fix this mess."

Crisis of Faith observed what little remained of his craft table. The man's work was in shambles, reduced to tender shards of brittle red clay scattered around in the dirt by her legs. She couldn't help but be impressed by how little it all amounted to: one tidy pile of fragments, barely three inches high. Folk Art buried his face in his hands.

"I'll make it up to you, I promise," she assured him. "I've been through things like this before." Folk Art rolled his eyes.

She got down on her hands and knees and began grasping at the broken shards, trying rather unsuccessfully to fit them back together.

"Forget it," he said, in a faraway voice. "I wasn't much good at pottery anyway. I should have quit while I was ahead. Everybody told me to stay in business school, to study finance or accounting, to work my way up to management, maybe get a job at my uncle's car dealership. But I went ahead and dropped out anyway, just to be my own boss. If I'm being honest with you, I don't even like pottery that much…"

Crisis of Faith didn't really hear that last part.

"You mean you dropped everything just to come out here, to the middle of nowhere, to be an *artist*?"

Folk Art frowned. "It's *not* the middle of nowhere. This region is known for its ceramic traditions, thousands of years—"

"Wow!"

Crisis of Faith began pacing back and forth in the dirt. Surely there was *something* they could do—an Artistically Inclined Business School Dropout and a Woman Suffering from a Crisis of Faith—to capitalize on their unlikely convergence of talents. She thought about something the teenager had said to her in the parrots' cave, something about fracking and exploitative mining and geopolitical fragmentation. She kicked at the table leg when the thought arrived to her and sent another three more bowls smashing.

"It seems you have frequent earthquakes in the area," she said.

"Yes. A big one ten years ago flattened half the town."

"Flattened!"

"Yes."

"Were there many deaths?"

"Yes, many deaths."

"Tourism gone too for a while, I suppose."

"Yes."

"And the pottery? Did any of it survive?"

Folk Art took a thoughtful pause. "Well, that's the beautiful thing about pottery, isn't it: the process, the failure. It's hard to be precious when you're working with clay."

"What happened to the pottery?" she asked again.

Folk Art shaded his eyes with one hand. Pointed to a little hill in the distance.

"Over there, where the old market used to be. Still in a pile, just colorful bits and shards…"

"*Shards*," she echoed.

Never mind the grief that came over Folk Art's face at the sound of that word, the immense and heavy sadness. She could not know it. The word sent her little thought gears whirring.

Working with broken pieces of things had always appealed to her, as a woman suffering from a crisis of faith. Putting little pieces of things into a state of order made her feel as if the world really could be put together again, right there, in her hands, even if only in a hypothetical way, and at a very small scale.

She got her phone out of her purse and flipped excitedly through a lengthy portfolio of images showcasing her homemade mosaic creations: assorted plates, tiles, vases, trivets, dog dishes, plant pots, picture frames, birdbaths... silly, cheerful things, by Folk Art's estimation, and shoddily executed.

"Well?"

Folk Art shrugged. "They're fine. Not great, but fine."

"*Fine*? Well, never mind. I'm going to need you to think outside the box. Think bigger..." Crisis of Faith cited Gaudí and Niki de Saint Phalle from knowledge gleaned from the covers of gallery catalogs and gift shop calendars. "What do you say," she said. "Our very own mosaic Tarot Garden, right here in the heart of Sierra Rota!"

Folk Art sucked at his lips for a while and released them. He looked, for the first time since she'd met him, rather like a businessman.

"You mean, like, charge admission and stuff?" he asked, straightening the collar of his shirt.

"Yes. It could be very lucrative."

"So people would come from all over the world..."

"Nothing less than a world-class attraction."

"And we could put up a concession serving tacos and American hamburgers..."

"I don't see why not."

"With games, like that one with the muscleman in Venice Beach, and the hammer...?"

They talked over the rest of the details, and soon it was settled. They would build a mosaic town on the site of the old market, and they would start work immediately.

They swept up the ceramic remains of Folk Art's stall with a broom and emptied the pieces into the plastic cooler. Then they set off up the road toward the hill where the rest of their raw materials lay.

For five months, the pair worked tirelessly from sunrise until sunset and sometimes right through the night packing bright little shards of glazed terra-cotta into their eclectic and very inspired designs. They took turns scavenging for tile and organizing it into colored piles, transporting water in plastic milk jugs from the creek that trickled down from the edge of the waterfall, and mixing up bucket after bucket of easy-blend mortar borrowed from a local construction site. It took some time to establish the foundations and skeletal structures, but once those were done, production was swift.

They built the houses first, each one with some signature American- or Mexican-style feature, with mosaic walls, mosaic window frames, mosaic chimneys, mosaic frescoes, mosaic bathtubs, mosaic grottoes, mosaic canopies, mosaic backsplashes, and intricate mosaic furniture and appliances. They built a mosaic cul-de-sac in the middle of all the houses, and in it, a circular mosaic medicine garden, complete with mosaic sundials and mosaic benches and mosaic interpretations of ancient agave. They built a mosaic playground with three swings and a slide, a mosaic school and a mosaic sports field, a mosaic auditorium for concerts.

They built a mosaic shopping mall with a mosaic Burger King and a mosaic Best Buy, and two grand mosaic highways full of mosaic gridlock leading toward it and away from it. They built a mosaic parking lot stretching as far as the eye could see; a fleet of decrepit mosaic city buses headed elsewhere, nowhere; a string of decrepit bus shelters leading away from them like crumbs.

They built a mosaic Old Quarter with quaint alleyways paved crookedly with mosaic, and mosaic boutiques with mosaic awnings and mosaic signage selling things like violins, slippers, and piñatas, all made up of mosaic. They built a lively mosaic pastelería at one end of the town and filled its windows with mosaic conchas and other pastries that lent themselves well to rendering in shards, while at the other end of the town, they built a mosaic art house cinema screening an indie romance chaotically rendered in mosaic, with a mosaic marquee, mosaic ticket booth, and mosaic tickets and popcorn.

They built a mosaic dog shelter and a mosaic soup kitchen for the benefit of the community. They filled the streets with mosaic shrubs, mosaic trash bins, mosaic drinking fountains and benches. They even built a mosaic dog run, and a mosaic version of one of those outdoor fitness circuits for seniors. Then they built a sculpture park (within their sculpture park) featuring enormous flowering mosaic jacaranda trees, and even more enormous mosaic sculptures of mythical animals built up and in and around them.

By the end of everything, they'd grown quite fond of each other's company. Crisis of Faith gushed about Folk Art's fine handiwork, while Folk Art complimented Crisis of Faith on her eye for design. They laughed together, kissed each other on the cheek. They called the mosaic village "their Empire."

By the end of everything, they were a little bit sorry for all that mosaic to end.

On the eve of the project's grand opening, Folk Art and Crisis of Faith went out for a celebratory dinner. They ordered grilled octopus and two gargantuan lime margaritas served in margarita glasses bigger than their heads. They ate chicken mole and shrimp, followed by another round of margaritas, and swallowed everything down with several pints of cold beer.

"To the good life!" Crisis of Faith toasted her companion.

Folk Art smiled and raised his glass. "To chance encounters!"

They drank cheerfully and Crisis of Faith was so happy and distracted that she didn't even notice the dog in her peripheral vision, canvassing a neighboring table for scraps. The boy from town came running onto the patio after it.

"Señora! Señora! It's here! The dog!" he cried, wanting very boldly to resecure the foreigner's affection.

Crisis of Faith shielded her eyes from this vision of her past self and continued her conversation, pretending not to recognize him. Eventually, the boy and the dog went away.

She never said anything more about this to Folk Art. Rather, after dinner, they wobbled out of the restaurant in each other's arms and back to Crisis of Faith's hotel room, where they made love for the first time, between paper-stiff maroon sheets, with great tenderness, awkwardness, and platonic trepidation. Afterward, Crisis of Faith rolled onto her belly and disclosed to him her one outstanding disappointment.

"I turn thirty on Friday, and I'm still waiting for my transformation. If it doesn't come soon, I'll have to wait another whole twenty-nine and a half years before my Saturn returns again…"

Folk Art tried to hide his subtle expression of hurt. Hadn't they just *made love*? And wasn't *making love*, in itself, *transformative*?

He put his personal feelings aside for a moment as he tried selflessly to convince her of her own recovery. They never could have achieved all that they had achieved, after all, without first overcoming all manner of physical, intellectual, and spiritual obstacle; all twelve steps on the ladder of introspection; all eighteen pillars of joy and acceptance; all twenty-one golden leaves of peace, self-love, gratitude, immersion; all fifteen purple arches of altruism, glee. Folk Art even used the trusty metaphor of a hungry caterpillar becoming cocoon becoming butterfly to illustrate the magnificent scale of her transformation. And still, Crisis of Faith disbelieved.

Her private crisis was simply not something a maker of folk art would ever—could ever—understand, she thought, as she listened politely but dispassionately to his beatitudes:

"That time you laid that shiny purple tile beside the green one and cried with satisfaction…"

"That time you held my hand at the top of the hill at sunrise and insisted…"

"That time you struck a gleaming pot clean in half with your bare fist…"

Folk Art was interrupted by the sound of a text message arriving on his phone. He fumbled around in the sheets to find it.

After a moment of quiet, she noticed he was crying.

"Somebody… Somebody's found my dog…" he stammered, rising trembling from the bed and jumping into his jeans. When the zipper on his fly jammed, he left it open and ran shirtless and barefoot out the door.

Crisis of Faith would never see him again.

Crisis of Faith lay in bed, one bare leg dangling off the side of it, as the sound of cicadas droned in through the open window, feeling, for the first time in her life, like the world was not a world, but an enormous, gaseous sphere—vaporous and impersonal, bigger than feelings—or at least, bigger than one person's idea of feelings—bigger than God and yet divinely accidental, huge and bright and not at all saturnine. She was, in that moment, not a woman, not a woman suffering at all, but just another mortal being lying randomly upon a sphere. Turning, turning, just another average human occurrence. *Here I am, right side up*, she thought dully. *Now here I am, upside-down.*

She put on her beige underwear, silk kimono, and slippers, and padded languidly out of the hotel room, swiping the cigarettes and matches Folk Art had left behind on her way out. Once outside, Crisis of Faith smoked and looked at the moon, its flat, asymmetrical face, and listened for a while to the hungry sound of stray dogs howling.

# TWENTY-THREE VERSIONS OF DISASTER

### 1

The boy yelled, "Earthquake!" when the earth split in two, suddenly finding his feet resting on two opposite ledges. Having many times been accused of having a split personality, he observed, on the one hand, dust and darkness and devastation, while on the other saw only mountain making and valley making and miracles.

### 2

First the walls, then the sink, then the paintings developed black mold. Then the mattress, then their sweaters, then their feet and ankles.

### 3

They called her unreliable and still, she tried to be a good employee.

### 4

A tropical storm came in on the horizon. All purple and swelling. Rain, and the smell of starfish washed up on the beach. One minute they were sopping, and then they were bopping. Bubbling, and then rotting. Then they were just rotten, and nude pink.

### 5

A man died in a plane crash, but really, he hadn't paid child support in years.

### 6

A girl felt a dark energy growing inside of her, but her psychiatrist was on holiday.

### 7

The Marxist bakers spat each day into the bread that was meant for the rich but that, unbeknownst to them, went each day to the poor.

### 8

She had gonorrhea and you had syphilis and I had chlamydia and he had herpes and they had yeast infections and we all secretly had HPV.

### 9

Heading home on his bike after the best race of his life, the competitive cyclist hit a stroller, then a motorbike, then a railing, then a pile of bricks, then a policeman, then a no-trespassing sign, then a colonial bust, then an antique cart full of used books and flowers—before being thrown, epically, into the canal.

## 10

Of two opposite and unspeakably violent acts committed in different places at exactly the same time: it could not be decided, when the respective cases finally went to trial, whether the wrongs should be squared or merely canceled out.

## 11

The shy, sensitive man slapped his big, strong wife and the next day, when she turned herself in, everyone believed her when she said she'd done it.

## 12

There was nothing anyone could ever do but set up tents outside the very buildings where they'd once afforded to live.

## 13

Somewhere a teenager attempted to take their own life based on a very common misunderstanding of Nietzsche.

## 14

The overachiever tried and tried and tried to get it up for the woman of his dreams, until finally the woman of his dreams got up to brush her teeth.

## 15

A tornado arrived just as the emerging writer was putting the finishing touches on their book. Afterward, there wasn't even anything they could do with the disordered pages: in that period post-Burroughs, post-Cortázar.

**16**

A curated famine wiped out the best of them while the worst of them ate well.

**17**

Both the baby monitor and the baby died in the night.

**18**

The radicalized young were prescribed amphetamines to ever dream of becoming president.

**19**

There was a massacre in the countryside that no one heard about.

**20**

A man blamed his mother for failing to prevent multigenre disaster.

**21**

An asteroid hit a part of Earth where only insects and small animals lived.

**22**

They might have been lovers, had either one had enough money.

**23**

They got all the way to the end before they realized they had failed.

## DREAMING AGAINST CAPITALISM

Things used to be simple. Before, before any of this happened, we used to doze off sweetly in little piles all over at lunch hour, and think, half dreaming, *There's a clogged drain over there, at the far end of the pond, and the moment someone gets around to unclogging it, I haven't the slightest idea how I'll make ends meet!*

We were resolved, at least, in our collective response to uncertainty.

*It must be lonely over there at the far end of the pond*, we thought glibly, upon waking. *It must be very cold...* We sipped dryly from the water glasses left over on our desks from the day before, the floating lint and mischievous hairs collecting around the corners of our mouths.

We tried to ready ourselves for the inevitable by picturing ourselves being sucked toward the dirty base of the drain, submitting to the downward current. We tried to picture ourselves swirling around inside the pipes, slowing our breathing like the daredevil Houdini in preparation for the impossible escape. (Each time, our imaginings were more heroic and far-fetched than the last—we always escaped just in time.)

In those days, we went to sleep without anyone telling us to. We fell asleep instantly out of genuine exhaustion from the sheer force of a day, far away from the clamor of calamities both in and outside of our control. We went to sleep without the idea of protest.

They gather us together around a circle of pillows. Tell us to lie down on our stomachs and picture the future flush with alternatives. Around us: melted-down credit cards poured into the molds of equity-sharing divinities, half-eaten bowls of rice sprinkled with the ashes of imperial fifty-dollar bills, power suits torn to rags and used to mop up the messes of our weeping.

We originally came here, most of us, because we either had time but no jobs and were hungry, or had jobs but no time and were unhappy. All of us, breaking anyway from the pressure to perform. Somewhere along the way we figured we'd been made sick by our own cult of optimization, and now we were too tired to innovate, too burnt to adapt.

Though unpaid like all the others, this internship at least presented a different kind of opportunity. A chance to join a cause. To be part of something bigger.

A man in blue coveralls raises his hand and asks whether we'll still have weekends where we're going.

"Shhhhh!" the collective hisses.

"But will we still be paid time and a half for holidays?" he wants to know.

*There will be no need to distinguish between weekdays and*

*weekends*, the glowing drain at the bottom of the pond replies. We let out a sigh of relief, returning our cheeks diligently to the imprints in our pillows.

I fantasize about the kinds of slumber parties I attended as a teen—pizza, gossip, group suspension—and practice inflating, deflating each one in my mind until all that's left is the concept. In truth, I want nothing more than to spend week after week in the comfort of my sheets, to fall asleep deeply and without consequence under the splayed pages of magazines, to grow up on the education of dreams.

But now my mother is calling me, my father is banging on the wall. Now, a child is crying, now a child is needing to be fed. I rummage around inside the cavity of my dreaming brain for crackers or a milk bottle as the crying gets louder and louder and the cavity fills up with garbage. I shuffle mistily through columns of babysitting certificates and energy drink cans in the vague direction of the bathroom, trip over a diaper bag on my way to the sink. I crack my jaw on the side of the toilet bowl and accidentally end up cleaning it.

By the time I look up again, it's almost morning.

The leaders encourage us, in our off time, to continue the cause. So all night long we build mazelike barricades in the street, transitioning eagerly from the sedation of our daytime sleep shifts into the chaos of organized nocturnal actions. We work vigilantly to obstruct the evening flow of consumers to restaurants, theaters, nightclubs, and airports with the heaps of our tidily rolled sleeping bags, cushioning charging vehicles and obscuring their sense of direction. Taxi drivers look confused as they're sent bouncing back in the direction from which they came. They've already been driving for days, even for nights, and now this. Will they still be paid for the trip?

We gather up our sleeping bags and hurry back to the pond in our striped satin uniforms and slippers in the early hours of the morning, excited about the progress we have made but increasingly unsure about whose side we are on. The shift worker? The sleeper? The activist? The capitalist? It hasn't yet occurred to us that we might really have been assigned the graveyard shift—that our activism and zeal for change have already been co-opted to perpetuate more of the same kind of exploitative labor from which we came. Dreaming as perpetual, hallucinatory antiwork work dream...What is left to be monetized but our very anger and dejection?

Dawn arrives but still, we are not yet permitted to sleep. We take off our socks and dip our toes into the cold weeds and mud, waiting patiently for the sound of the steel triangle to ring out across the pond, signaling the start of our next dream.

The clogged drain shudders but does not let up.

The water in the pond is the color of bird shit: green with streaks of white, or white with streaks of green, and when I think of all the things that could be trapped in it, my head screams with fear.

Ming wants to take drugs and dive to the bottom of the pond to investigate, but I'm frightened and quite possibly still dreaming so I refuse. Eli is sleeping soundly with the others, and I'm afraid of leaving him behind.

They tell us that the punishment for refusing to sleep from nine to five, Monday to Friday, is a liter of pond water down the throat. Likewise if you are found to be donning any other uniform but the satin one you are given. All of this, it is explained, is to withdraw our standardized labor from the standard workday, to slow down the flow of capital into a market that does not serve us. The leaders in our group, it turns out, have already drunk their share of pond water—mostly during their time as CEOs and COOs and CFOs of powerful multinational corporations. We try to ask them what led them to join the revolution, but they are evasive. Instead, they show us the calluses on the insides of their cheeks as a warning, making sure to do this right before bedtime.

"Drink gunk in your dream life and you'll never have to drink it in real life," they tell us assuredly. This, they say, is what gives them their edge.

I used to deliver pizzas, first by bike, and then by car. I used to lift elderly people on and off toilet seats, and children on and off slides. I worked for a while in a warehouse packing perfume samples into gift boxes, and then at another warehouse arranging pallets of animal feed on shelves. I worked as a waiter at a karaoke bar (code for after-hours janitor at a karaoke bar), and then just long enough as a dishwasher in the kitchen of a wedding caterer to develop mysterious blotches on my face and arms from the steam. The last place I worked was at a customer-service call center, answering questions about a dangerous weight-loss drug that made everyone feel poorly. All of them I quit with less zeal than the last.

I used to lie down on the floor beneath my call center cubicle, curled up on a bed of carpet so tight and gray that I developed psychosomatic asthma. My coworkers would trip over my legs when they passed and ask what I was doing. "Just taking a quick power nap," I'd lie, followed by the assurance that I'd be twice as productive in twenty minutes when I awoke. "Trust me," I said, "the science says…"

Repeat after us:
> *I've been asleep for years, and it is a privilege!*
> *I haven't the slightest idea how to make ends meet!*

I am brought up like a horse, and receive just enough to enable me to work:
> Flat black shoes for gripping the earth.
> Oatmeal for energy and water for high-functioning organs.
> A sliver of sunlight for skin.
> A single bed the height of a trough.
> ~~An expensive phone with which to call my lover.~~
> A dark, secluded place to shit.

In one recurring dream, I can be found scouring the shelves of some labyrinthine library looking for clues as to the sleep habits of Karl Marx. I want to know about the man's personal relationship to work and sleep and leisure. I want to get a sense of the consistency of his days.

Did he sleep well, or hardly at all? Did he rise monastically before dawn each morning to do his important work, then continue at it diligently into the night? Or did he in fact sleep lazily until noon and rise foggy headed, writing in short bursts and only when he felt like it? Secretly, of course, I'm hoping he was less high functioning than he seemed.

Did he sleep with a quill in his hand, behind the ear (always working), or did he scratch his manifestos impulsively into the back of his hand with a twig? Are we so sure that a more well-rested lover or assistant didn't just quietly assemble, correct, and transcribe his sentences while he was sleeping, creating and re-creating each word as their own? Was the lonely labor of each word really his, or not a labor at all? Didn't he ever fall asleep under the weight of his own thinking?

I feel my way around to the outer corner of the library and find myself lingering there by an open window, afraid to reenter the stacks. From this great distance the biographies appear so thick, and the shelves so impossibly psychedelic, that I'm no longer sure I have what it takes.

They summon us just after nine p.m. and ask us to gather round the grassy side of the pond. We've been sleeping in longer and longer, it seems, the wake-time triangle delayed by fifteen minutes each day so that now when we rise it is already well after nightfall. Tonight, the moon is full and bright and is asking to be read to, they tell us.

Samantha goes first, reading from a secondhand textbook on neoliberalism. She reads from a random page in the chapter called "The New Modern Economics" then rips it from the book and throws it into the reeds. "Fuck the gig economy!" she shrills. "Fuck deregulation! Fuck lezee fair! Fuck supply and demand!"

The crowd roars up in whistles and hoots.

Next comes Eva in her robotic tone, reading a long list of dental ailments that pain her but that she cannot afford to fix. "Abscess in three, thirteen, sixteen. Gingivitis on four, twenty-nine, seven, nine. Periodontitis, cracked crown, withering alveolar bone…" Her descriptions rattle across the cold surface of the pond. When she's done, she rips the list clean in half and sets the two halves floating along the water's edge. The paper floats, then eventually sinks, while the rest of us stand around solemnly, bowing our heads.

Marc details the going price for canvas and tubes of oil paint and all the other things preventing him from being an artist. "The only thing left," he says, "is to make art about the very conditions of lacking. The only remaining relevant thing…"

*You're the lucky one among us,* some of us think but don't say.

He's right about the only remaining relevant thing.

When it gets to be my turn, I realize that I have not prepared—I haven't brought anything to read. I look up at the moon for inspiration, and, luckily for me, the moon growls back:

*Only so long as you are working. And you are healthy. And you are normal…*

I get down on my hands and knees and claw at the dirt, beginning in a melodramatic whisper and crescendoing into a screech:

"Only so long as I am *working*—and not unemployed—am I *worthy*!"

"Only so long as I am *healthy*—and not sickly—am I *sound*!"

I throw pond water down my throat and smear my face with mud, just to show myself most desperate and incredulous.

"Only so long as I am *normal*—and not sleeping, not eating, not loving, not making—"

"Only so long as I am *not making a fuss*—"

"Only so long as I don't blame the *system*, but only blame *myself*—"

"Only so long as I'm *okay* with *working hard* and doing *more* with *less*—"

"Only so long as I'm not lying at the *bottom* of the ladder, but not exactly *climbing* it either—"

I rip off my clothes as the group screams in ecstasy. I dive into the pond and the group follows after me, all of us swishing around ravenously in the twisted reeds. I gather the dirty pond water in my mouth and rise up like a wild yeast, my arms outstretched, before releasing the water slowly over the shelf of my lips, my head swirling with the adrenaline of lifelong betrayal.

I dream that I am running away from the library of failed research on Marx and out into an empty street. Nobody around. It is raining gently, and the wet satin sticks to my thighs. My feet pad limply at the pavement, my slippers becoming ever more waterlogged as I go.

I'm groggy from sleep, but alert on another plane. My fingertips extend in all directions and become the pinpricked flesh of the city, busy cataloging its phantom limbs. *This* public lamppost, *this* public street sign, *this* public toilet, *this* public garbage bin. *That* private lobby, *that* private parking lot, *that* private elevator, *that* private topiary hedge.

O haunted skyscraper that could house ten thousand but prefers to house no one!

O silver skyline! O vacant public square!

To whom do you belong?

In this city clogged with ambition, collared with workers, blue with sleep. In this city, the sun is rising.

I emerge at noon from my sleep shift with a bad headache and the limpness of an overrested body. My stomach sags from the spine, the doughy muscles in my legs having reverse engineered into those of an infant's. At the beginning, we adhered to a strict sleep regimen—eight hours a day, no more, no less, lest one should become overtired and unable to perform—but now our sleep shifts run twelve, fourteen, sixteen hours each day. It's become quite difficult to discern the contours of a clock.

"Perform, but in what way?" we ask our leaders, yawning.

"Shhhhh!" the executives reply in unison.

Even sleeping now feels like working! Even napping feels like gigging!

Karla points to the new convertible they have parked on the street, cleverly covered up with reeds, and asks what convertibles have to do with the revolution.

"Shhhhh!" the executives reply once more, this time indignant.

Bobby, growing suspicious, decides to press further.

"What is it exactly that you get up to all day anyway, while we're so busy sleeping?" The clogged drain gurgles, releasing tiny bubbles to the surface. "I mean, how do we even know that you're really sleeping when we're sleeping—and not secretly running some double shift?"

Little by little, unrest brews by the pond.

I awake one night and find myself alone, the others having left me behind for the barricades. Somewhere by my body, a friendly animal is breathing; I find myself drifting pleasantly in and out of sleep with its breath as a metronome:

I dream about the stress of a working day.

I dream about the stress of precarious pay.

I dream that I have been relegated forever to the night shift.

I dream about reading a magazine in bed on a Saturday.

I dream about drinking coffee in convertibles with reclining seats.

I dream about what it would be like to change the world through a series of small but repetitive turns.

I dream about the dream of collective action and results.

I dream about buying property so that I can lie down on it.

I dream about receiving an unadvertised honorarium at the end of my internship.

I dream about going to bed at exactly the same time as everybody else—what feels like practically an erotic fantasy, these days—until I wake up sweating and even more alone.

Across the pond, the city wakes and stirs, swishing its little lights and engines. I trudge through the mud to an old pine canoe and get into it, pushing off from the edge with a rotting paddle. I paddle as hard as I can to the center of the pond, then lie down on my back across the seats and close my eyes. Dreaming awake, I float and float.

There's a story in these parts about the people who are sleeping. That we sleep all day because we are privileged. That we sleep all night too because we are anxious, dopey, romantic. That we act like we have no friends, when we do; that the water has made us hypersensitive and of poor humor. That we are theatrically naive, and naively theatrical. That our political commentary is so literal it pains them.

But to our detractors, we ask you this: Would you really prefer we do nothing? Would you really prefer that we take what little we are given and say, *Okay, Capitalism, I have seen your gaping maw, and I want no trouble with you*?

The revolution may be imperfect, but we remain committed. We fail, we fall back, we regroup, we adapt. We try again.

Back at the camp, Eli holds my hand in the night and tells me he is afraid of the dark. We've been living outdoors for so long now that I would have thought he would have long become accustomed to being in it, even if it meant we never really got to feel the sun on our retinas. I can sense that he is growing, changing, in ways that make him wiser than me and therefore cast me as more monstrous. I wonder about the architecture of our resistance and what it's done to our sense of trust, of closeness, of rest. What it's done, even, to our sense of wealth.

We are prescribed sleep all day and all night now, spritzed with pond water each time we attempt to open our eyes. Our bodies are so soft now many of us can no longer remember how to move. Still, we do our best to harness new powers: focusing our minds on the intensive training of our dreams toward bigger and more brilliant futures. No one quite predicted, of course, the extent to which all this dreamwork would also serve to sharpen our imaginations—intensifying our deepest and most personal fears as much as our collective capacities for magical thinking.

Through my eyelids, I overhear the leaders talking about the coming end. Something about the need for better metrics, refreshed tactics, a change of schedule, personnel. I am overcome by the violent desire to slash open my sleeping bag and run to them, screaming; to grab hold of their shoulders and shake them until they wake. How much will we be owed, and what will be due, when the next bell sounds?

I float until I hit the shore.

## A JOURNEY, SOME RICHES, SOME CASTLES, SOME GARBAGE

He met her in the alley and handed her a napkin. Told her they had some important business to attend to.

"What kind of business?" she asked, her eyes dumb like lozenges. The napkin was so greasy it was hard to see the map on it.

He asked her what she would do with a million dollars.

"I never wanted to be ri—" she started, but her imagination betrayed her: already, on her tongue, the goodness of a ripe peach in winter, and the soft spray of one of those showerheads designed to reproduce the feeling of rain. He touched her arm lightly, her arm without a coat in the night, and she trusted him but only because the page said, *Trust*. Someone from one of the neighboring brewpubs wheeled a container of fresh trash out onto the street, emptied the bags into the dumpster, and came back out a second time wheeling a grease can.

"Again!" the Director shouted. "From the top!"

They pretended not to hear. Her companion pointed at a concrete fortress way up on the hill. They would break in under the new moon, he said. They would break in tonight.

She looked up at the dilapidated building meant somehow to impress her, thinking how sometimes it is good to see these things, up close and personal—if not to understand them, exactly, then just to add depth to the things that you know. She blinked slowly as people in black T-shirts pushed the alley away by holding on to its edges, swapping it for someone's artistic interpretation of woods.

They packed some sesame snaps for the journey and headed out on the dirt path toward the castle. The trail was dark and thin and full of owls. What is it about language that's always wanting to have its way, drawing things so simply in some places and so complicatedly in others?

An hour later they realized they'd been circling the castle for days.

She scrunched the napkin into a ball and threw it over the far side of the mountain before retreating around a nearby tree trunk to think. Her companion took an irreverent piss on the mossier side.

She got out a pen and notebook from her bag and began sketching the shapes of small animals she imagined crinkling above her. There was this project she'd been working on at home that she still meant to return to. A project that required also the prereading of a specific book she had been meaning to get to on mountain painting and abstraction. What was the name of it again? Doesn't matter. It was possible that it had long been reduced to shreds anyway by the scavenging kinds of birds or else the teeth of her baby daughter.

"Cut! I said cut!"

She flipped the page and began sketching some thudding

animals below. The problem with following maps is that they can be made by just about anyone, right, and there's no one on the planet who can be trusted with such a task. No one on the planet who really has that kind of higher-up-enough view to say, *This way for sure*. Not even the Director knows! Not even the Director/God, who *pretends* to know but not say—

She closed her notebook and went back around to the other side of the tree to confront her companion with a clear string of words. They were so busy arguing in the scene and scenes after that they never even noticed the artist approach, freshly drunk on free wine tapped from the castle cellar.

"Hey there," he said. "Which way to town? I promised to fetch one more painting and install it in the castle lobby before sunrise!" He was dressed in a royal-purple robe, what looked at first like heavy velvet but turned out to be fleece, a bathrobe.

They approached him cautiously and circled, sharklike.

"You've just come from the castle?"

The artist grinned and gestured sloppily in the direction from which he'd come. There, in the moss, there appeared a small door. They leaped toward it, but not before the artist had managed to fall, laughing, to the ground, grabbing hold of her right ankle and coiling his big, drunk body around it.

"I'm just so...*tired*," he said, gripping tighter, as she dragged the heavy appendage through the ferns, another reason to fear theater. *But there's good theater, and there's bad theater*—she didn't buy it. They pushed open the door and found themselves in the greenroom.

The artist did a little twirl between the bulky couches, beaming with pride and recognition. He then retrieved a hammer from the ground and began banging a long nail into the wall. It was met with some resistance.

"You told me there'd be *treasure*," she whispered to her associate, trading in the title of "companion" for something chillier and more businesslike to symbolize both her loss of trust and her personal desire for better boundaries as a result of it. "You told me we'd be *rich*."

She inventoried the perimeter of the greenroom, tripping over secondhand coffee mugs and extension cords, looking for some hidden door that would reveal to her the *real* castle, the one full of antique lutes and jewels. Of course the chamber was sealed tight as can be, windowless and subterranean, how could it be otherwise, there are no guarantees in this world, with no way out but back the way they came. She went gloomily to a couch at the back of the room and sat down beside a disgruntled teenage stagehand who was swigging peach cooler from a plastic two-liter jug.

"Have you ever thought," the stagehand waxed, "about just how *odd* the shape of a bottle is…how *odd* the inverted shape of the glass…and how *like* the shape of the human mind…" They had a persuasiveness about them that suggested they would one day become a great actor.

"Do you mean you *like* their oddness?" she asked. The stagehand was twirling the heavy jug by its tiny neck with their fingertips. They eventually offered her some.

"Just look at how unevenly the logic is applied," the stagehand continued. "Some things look like they were very carefully thought out, while others look like they were made very quickly, under duress, by someone with zero experience."

"Do you mean you find their unevenness unreliable?" she asked, taking the bottle from them.

"I mean, if this one thing's accidental, then who's to say the rest isn't too?"

"Do you mean you think most shapes are amateur?" she pressed on.

"What's accidence and what's coincidence…" the stagehand continued.

"Do you mean is it better or worse to think things through?"

She watched as the stagehand lowered their heavy, mascaraed lashes down over the ledge of their cheeks and hoisted them back up again, over and over, like a drawbridge. She watched this lowering and hoisting for what felt like an eternity, until nothing was left in the jug, until they were done talking and practically asleep. Then she pinched herself to come back out.

She'd just about had it with this journeying, she thought, with its castles and noncastles and treasures and nontreasures. A castle, it turns out, is just another city dump, story mixed in with nonstory mixed in with language and its rebuttals. Combustible heroes. Combustible monologues. Combustible poems.

She searched the room for the person she'd come with only to find him teetering around on the floor with the artist in his arms, conjoined by the fleece bathrobe. She tried to do something outrageous to get their attention—or, better, to end the play—but the two took no notice of her.

"Death to theater!" she found herself shouting, even though it was ridiculous, theater would never die, and when they continued to ignore her, she grabbed an empty wine bottle from the floor and threw it against the farthest wall. To her delight, the wall tore open like paper, because it was. She leaped triumphantly into the hole.

"Adieu!" she cried, diving headfirst into the tunnel behind it. When her exit went unnoticed, she came back in through the hole she'd made and tried it again. "Toodle-oo!" she said. Nothing. "Ta-ta!" she tried once more. Finally, a custodian entered from the wings and waved goodbye.

She followed the tunnel as far as it would go. She followed the tunnel forever into the center of the earth, only to arrive at the end of the set and find that it too held nothing.

She put down the broken bottle neck she'd been clutching for her protection and slumped to the floor.

*What happened to effort + effort + effort = reward...* she thought, her head filling with the disintegrating images of peaches and rain. Somewhere, elsewhere, whole industries were collapsing. She hoped next time it might be hers.

# A BRIEF HISTORY OF FEELING

### Ecstasy

500 billion years ago—The dark touches itself in the dark and experiences something like ecstasy. Except that ecstasy isn't a feeling yet—the sensation is just kind of sharp and warm. Afterward, the dark feels happy and breathless. Afterward, the dark feels lonely.

### Hunger

4.6 billion years ago—A depressive speck of dust eats everything in the refrigerator until it is planet sized and still wanting more. It wants and wants and vibrates around the universe, eating up everything in its path, plus more. The less filling things are the only things left now, the only things safe now: those empty shards, those empty half-moons, stars.

### Curiosity

3.7 billion years ago—A bolt of lightning strikes a rock and cracks it clean open, like an axe into a durian, like a tender karate chop into a walnut. Inside, there is something stringy and green, something that needs to be pried from its shell in order to be properly examined. Luckily, this activity makes for challenging and deeply satisfying work. Luckily, this activity goes on for eternity.

### Attraction

2 billion years ago—Two organisms kiss, and need no oxygen, none at all.

### Jubilation

400 million years ago—What is jubilation but the possibility of loving everything and at the same time?

### Injustice

250 million years ago—A thousand baby ferns poke out of the dirt and battle for sunlight and the right to grow. They are told they are all equal and exactly the same and that no one has an unfair advantage over the other, even though it's obvious that some of them have extralong arms, and some have louder personalities, or more loving parents.

### Forsakenness

120 million years ago—The very first and most beautiful flower in the world lies wilting at one hundred thousand meters above sea level, having been plucked by an invisible force and thrown into the snow. The feeling: futility, and the first expression of waste.

### Persistence

50 million years ago—The manufacture of a popular tourist beach. I can't quite picture it, can you, each singular, exotic, spotted shell, the smooth of it, the sheer grit of it, its top side, its underside, just turning and turning and turning and turning and turning itself, in this gentlest of epochs, in this slowest of factories, into a most luxurious brand of sand.

### Spontaneity

14 million years ago—A barnacle kisses a donkey and takes her from behind.

### Generosity

4.59 million years ago—Two organisms, still kissing, stumble in their reverie upon a stranger smoking out in the cold. The stranger wears a fleece coat and leans drunkenly into the wind; the stranger is the first stranger they've ever seen. They approach him with trepidation and small offerings of pine cones. They offer him coffee, even though their home is very small.

### Love

3 million and 1 years ago—A woman holds her newborn in the dark, and feels enormous love for the thing she herself made, but cannot, at that moment, see.

### Rage

200,000 years ago—A man picks up a rock and throws it through the window of the world.

## JACQUELYN ZONG-LI ROSS

### Speechlessness

140,000 years ago—The arch moves the knee moves the hip moves the cheek moves the heart moves the lung moves the throat moves the tongue and makes the lips quiver, *buh buh puh muh fuh duh duh duh duh.* The worst part about narration is the worst part about speech. *Ay ee ai oh yu.* Back turned to the curtain, who even knows what I mean? And still, refusing to sing. The worst part about voicing is the heavy gesture. The moodiness of the hollow.

### Wonder

10,000 years ago—A mother calls her daughter calls her uncle calls her cousin and everyone gathers around a metal bowl. She fills it with warm water and they kneel down next to it, everybody closing their eyes. One of them sings into it. Another runs their finger around the rim. Another one sends wreaths of daisies floating. Until a kind of miracle occurs, and the first one to recognize it calls it out.

### Angst

6,309 years ago—A boy refuses, like the donkey, to be made to go. "He's going through a period of intense individualization," they say, of the boy who no longer speaks and only looks forlornly across the sand. "He's going through a period of necessary rebellion." The boy strokes the hair of the donkey, the only one who understands him, and questions the moon and the almost-moon and the stars. The people assemble a giant clock on the hillside, and wait for the cloud to pass.

### Rejection

5,000 years ago—The familiar dark rubs itself against the peak of a pyramid, edging toward that old friend, ecstasy. In the final seconds before orgasm, the dark pauses in enjoyment, but the pyramid remains sullen and distant and silent.

### Vanity

2,500 years ago—A civilization pines over poetry and fine pottery, and this is the expression of the original lust. We collapse hillsides and wage small wars with language. We trade old poems for shinier, more class-confirming ones. We trade perfectly good pots for ones that illustrate a greater mastery of fire.

### Skepticism

2,000 and some years ago—I'm told the heavens crack open and an impossible grace runs all over the plate. It's messy and ideological, gets all over stuff. It makes the masses both more tender and more violent. It attempts to qualify the end.

### Melodrama

1,300 years ago, exactly—A princess in a castle, surrounded by servants and rooms, agrees to meet her eligible bachelors. When the day finally arrives, however, the princess is in a mood. She refuses to bathe. She orders platters of grapes to her room. She glares with vengeance at the sea—and this mood is a thing she cannot, or else refuses to, explain.

### Senselessness

800 years ago—The newborn, once so loved by its mother, is now a man. One day the loved man is conscripted to go to war, and the whole way there he thinks, *What a senseless thing, how horrific, that I should go and take another man's head, and that if I don't, that man'll have mine!* He goes, but keeps his eyes closed the whole time. He takes blind jabs at enemies, holding the sword in his left

hand. He walks backward toward the firing line. He refuses to partake in a violence that is anything less than random because randomness is the only thing keeping him from cruelty.

### Ignorance

470 years ago—The stranger is outside the house again, this time cursing wildly about the coming end. We do not invite him in. Instead, we call him a heretic, a lunatic, a fruit loop. We close the blinds. We turn on the TV. He makes a grand mess of the lawn with his pacing, all his mindless chatter about worlds and spheres.

### Alienation

250 years ago—A great sadness presses itself against the belly of the city. It burps black smoke and fog, making it difficult to see your neighbors. A mother goes to work before sunrise and returns at three; a father goes to work at three and returns just after sunrise. Rabid dogs all over the street. The bread there goes stale within the hour.

### Liberation

50 years ago—The good people assemble, en masse, by the pond. They raise words on sticks and stomp their feet. They call out those in high towers of power. Everybody makes love and defends their right to make it. A man kisses a man and takes him from behind.

### Humiliation

35 years ago—In a bathroom stall, the sudden impossibility of owning anything, music so loud you no longer recognize your body, no longer know the right way to be aroused. Years and minutes spent in the stench of perspiration, in the violation that moves glitter around on your cheeks, glitter whose only purpose

is to render sadly illuminated those tough balls of want, your psychic disintegration—touch, like a burrowing tapeworm; toilet like an open clam.

### Anxiety

25 years ago—We hold hands on the porch at midnight and make a wish for the new millennium. For money, health, vacations, family, success, mindfulness, luck, sex, affection, grace, tenderness, compatibility, ambition, time, beauty, faith, gratitude, memory, fallibility, courage, clarity, good fortune, mobility, strength, confidence, motivation, respect, humility, creativity, inspiration, grounding, focus, safety, spaciousness—and speed, oh, speed because we may not live tomorrow and we are running out of time.

### Confusion

18 years ago—I walk into the room and feel at once too young and too old. I take a seat at the bar and grunt like an old man, swing my legs from the stool like a young one. Someone behind me calls me baby, and I think, either I really am somebody's baby again or else I must be somebody's whore. I don't know anymore which one I am, or which version of myself I prefer to be.

### Optimism

A year ago—Imagine, the angle of the light, just right. You have enough money. Your heart is bursting. You throw all your old work into the dumpster and start anew beside a bowl of ripe mango because suddenly you have too many good ideas. You run into the yard and mow the lawn. You mow your neighbor's lawn too because you are kind. You write letters to your friends proposing epic performances and activations. You pick all the clothes up off the floor.

### Pessimism

Last week—We're told, we narrowly avoid death. Being blown up on the subway. Drowning in the Mediterranean Sea. We have no rights. We are not safe. We have no bodies, no intellectual or emotional future. We collect empty cans from the ditch. We are con artists and poultry workers. We are gamblers and custodians. We are undertakers and squatters and refugees. Truth is a word we've heard used, but don't use. Scarcity is a word we use.

### Regret

Just yesterday—I watch as a long-legged spider wobbles into a paper cup and stays there a while, before wobbling away. I crush it with a rolled-up magazine on its way to the window, and scrape its thin body into the trash can.

**TIGER BALM**

*What kind of research is the most dangerous kind of research?*

Q stands by the window, fanning herself with a long, iridescent peacock feather that she found, a long time ago, on the floor of a shopping mall. She's just applied eucalyptus oil to her neck and crooked right leg, and now the fanning motion pushes the smell around the room, blending confusedly with the aromas of steam buns and foul-smelling standing shower water that floods the bathroom floor and for some reason eternally refuses to drain, preferring instead to wrap itself around the base of the toilet, the broken plunger, the pedestal sink, the trash can full of shit-covered toilet paper. Q scrunches her nose and puts down the feather, traipsing in her pink plastic slippers and cane to the bathroom. There she empties the contents of the trash into a plastic bag and takes the stinking bundle out to the alleyway.

It's morning and this kind of alleyway only ever smells like piss in the morning. No escaping the stench. In the afternoon, it's gasoline. Every twenty-four hours men fall out of the soup joint at one end and pile into the car mechanic's shop at the other. Smashing bottles all down the way. Then smashing wrenches. Loud as hell. That is, if the fires don't get to them first.

*If the fires, and the thieves, and the ghosts don't get to them…*

Q tries not to wish bad things upon anybody, but privately, she does wish them upon a few. Hard not to, really, when the elsewhere-wish can't be helped, whether or not she is wishing anything upon anyone. Does this make her monstrous?

Q doesn't believe in spells, but if she did.

If she did, she'd say, *This city is under some kind of spell…*

Q rounds the corner of her apartment building in the direction of the dumpster, grease squishing up the toes of her shoes. Her bad leg drags, the rubber sole of that shoe folding and unfolding against the gravel like a piece of ham. Beside her, a band of wild cats stretch out along the gutter. A row of pried-open tuna cans lie rotting just beyond them in the shade of some scrubby bushes.

Q glances over her shoulder. Nobody around but her.

"Tiger," she whispers to the biggest, fattest one, "you're much too sweet to live among us on this dirty, dirty Earth. If I were you, I'd get lost quick!"

Tiger looks at her stonily, then blinks once and yawns: claws appearing then disappearing into the pads of his paws.

Q tosses her trash bag into the dumpster's open corner, where it lands soundlessly at the exact moment that a stranger manifests around the dumpster's opposite side.

"I'm looking for a little shop," the man says, pacing. "One I visited when I was a child."

He is wearing a green hat. Q does not trust him.

"It had a red awning," he continues. "And a sign that read either *medicine* or *massage*."

Q shrugs and points vaguely in the direction opposite the sun. Just to be rid of him. Sending him as far away as Neptune, Pluto. It strikes her as quite stupid, to be looking for anything, never mind from one's childhood. Nothing ever is as it once was.

"I can only assume it's burned down then," he says, looking at his feet.

The man exhales a long, wheezing string of syllables, spits on the ground, and leaves.

*Can a balm be more than maybe-medicine? Can a balm be stronger than juice?*

The lucky ones will come down with it mildly: a faint rash on their left wrist, making them unusually vulnerable to pickpocketing. The unlucky ones though will find the rash spreading quickly across their body, bringing with it not only the usual thievery, but also: unexplained kitchen fires, menacing terrors in the night. The rash will become itchier and itchier. Itchier and itchier and also more uncouth. Add to that the stench of an ever-present smoke. Then: the fear of being broke. Broker than broke, wrapping itself around the inside of the thigh. Moving up into the pubic bone, the armpit, the lip. Gone behind the ear. The tremor of being forever a victim.

Q, being thus far spared, spends her long days investigating topical remedies for the town's maladies, not out of care for those affected, but in order to secure her own immortality. She's tired, after all, of hearing her neighbors say, "Oh, there goes poor, pretty Q with her fake limp, who doesn't have to do hard labor for a living…" or, "Oh, there goes Q with her makeup and crutches and useless degree in poetry…" *Surely it is possible to research something to life, just as it is possible to research it to death,* she thinks. She tells herself this inside the logic of her most perfect, imperfect, most mortally fashioned questions, of which she has so many. Where did she come from? And where is "here"? She is convinced that her research will be not only topical, but transportive.

Q's research leads her into the deepest of online forums, where, awash in blue light into the early hours, she collects new formulations of ancient ingredients and reads about their purported health benefits. Despite being trained in neither chemistry nor traditional medicine, Q shows a strong aptitude for the work. Her clicking finger quivers; the sun rises and sets.

She is looking for the perfect balm.

It is late autumn. Outside under the smoke-pink moon that shuffles from one end to the other end of the same mountain range without ever leaving, the trees shudder and drop their leaves. Q goes to the post office to collect her latest samples: a heap of powerful and strongly scented packages sent from addresses hardly locatable in the mind. Returning home, her bag is so heavy she has to stop halfway to catch her breath. She braces her cane against the curb and gets out her paper fan. Cardamom. Menthol. Skunk cabbage. Dollar store perfume. The men at the nearby bar meanwhile teeter around on their stools and laugh.

"Oh, look," one man pronounces loudly to his friends. "It's Princess Q all dressed up for a banquet! I wonder what she does with all those parcels. What do you think she could be hiding in there?"

"I bet she's got some foul ingredients for her soup pot—"

"I bet she's got herself some fine lotions for her dry patches—"

"I bet you she's sending her dirty panties all over the internet—"

"Hey, Q!" another one yells. "You have a date tonight?" The man gets up from his stool and unzips his fly. All the men laugh and clink their bottles as Q silently pockets her fan and continues on her way.

*If I blend sense and nonsense, will it result in a more beautiful medicine?*

Things Q slathers on her bad leg, by order of application: pureed ginseng, cilantro, pomelo, cloves, diaper cream, crushed walnuts, sugarcane, melted refrigerator ice, bathwater, gutter water, spring water, bottled water, grated ginger, soy milk, cow milk, cum, coconut oil, trampled birch bark, rock-sugar syrup, honey, black tea, green tea, molasses, compost, soft tofu, jojoba oil, coffee grounds, winter melon, bitter melon, watermelon, other kinds of melon, orange peel, trampled hawthorn berries, laundry soap, rose perfume, sesame oil, chrysanthemum flowers, pulverized fresh breath mints, frankincense, beeswax, daisy petals, baby lotion, cigarette ash, dried mackerel, dust, mashed banana, mangosteen...

*If only a balm were not a balm but a medium for portaling...*

Ten days later, the man with the green hat comes knocking, and loudly, on the lower door of her apartment building. It is late, a quarter past eleven. Not a songbird in the street. The elderly landlady on the first floor answers first, throwing open the shutters of her kitchen window to scold him.

"What's wrong with you?" she yells through the bars.

Q gets up from her computer and walks over to the window in her plastic slippers, drawing back the curtain a sliver to observe the scene below. It is snowing lightly. The branches of the peach tree are bare and dusted with white.

"Please," the man is saying, sobbing, "I've been robbed."

"Who robbed you?"

"A band of giant cats, miss, each one bigger than a tiger!"

"Cats!"

"They took everything—my money, my family jewelry, even the dried fish from my pantry. I only know it was them because I caught sight of their tails waving at me down the alleyway…" The man raises his arms to demonstrate with a fierce, waving motion. Q observes a faint rash on his left wrist. "Please…"

The landlady shakes her head and sullenly closes the shutters, leaving the man outside in the cold.

Q watches him for a while, his small figure slumped against the naked tree, the snow dusting the tops of his worn-out sneakers. He looks rather like an older version of a boy she went to high school with—a boy she went to high school with in another life. She wonders whether this boy likes poetry like the other one did. Whether this one too has a thing for iambic pentameter. Wasn't he right, at least, about language being the most accessible kind of magic. And about it being possible, after all, to make a wish and bring about a change—

Q closes the curtain and returns to her computer, rubbing her aching leg. Somehow, she knows, this man is the type of man best left alone.

*What is the best temperature for balm making?*

Poetry at the warming hour. Impatience at three. Four forty-five and tepid in the possibility of everything being solved, resolved. Mortality setting in, mortality setting in. Seconds adding up to minutes adding up to hours adding up to days. Ten degrees Celsius in the balm of a decade's mildest winter, in which everything arrives already thawed. Downstairs landlady knocking about the failing bathroom pipes, water collecting in the ceiling of her shower stall. Ten, fifteen, twenty degrees and a snapshot of breath rising in a cool room. Draw the curtains to preserve the best conditions for balm making: warm and dim, the electric baseboard heater blowing upward on the lowest setting. Twenty-three degrees now and the very best temperature for balm making. About the drip that never fails. Nine o'clock and looking for love; nine fifteen and already retreating, wounded. The loss of feeling your mind and body slipping before your time. Mottled aromas condensing in sticky patches on the walls.

*Instructions for Research-Creation Against Fires, Thieves, Ghosts:*

1. Make your rounds of the tubs. Turn each mixture once into itself with a porcelain spoon. Remove any developing mold from the surface.
2. Jot down the date, texture, and smell of the contents of each tub. Describe its closest color. Write all of this down in your spiral-bound notebook, the one you always keep open on your nightstand. Resharpen your pencil.
3. Pulverize the fresh ingredients in a blender. Pulverize them to a fine iridescent pulp, and do not be afraid. Place whatever results in a new tub. Label it with its date, time, fear, and motivation.
4. Go into the bathroom and slather the new substance all over your leg. Add your custom sense notation to the

jotting. Tingling, burning, cooling, etcetera. Add your custom desires. Inscribe them in the balm with your thumb, against the leg that refuses.

5. Speak to the balm. Disclose to it whatever comes to mind. Fleshy or inchoate. Legible or illegible. Speak to it as the medium it is, a carrier.
6. Elevate your feet. Close your eyes. Work hard, in the way of the best, most effervescent exfoliant, to shed matter and mind…
7. …Heat and antiheat. Heart and antiheart. Material and antimaterial. Jot down what you find there, in the spirit of open research.
8. Impersonate the sneering men at the bar, role-playing your better future responses:
   "…nets of respiratory viruses to fog your lungs—"
   "…an everlasting gray rot to wilt your spirit—"
   "…aborted manuscripts, all your good ideas—"
   "…dampness to follow you to heaven and to hell—"

(The smell is strongest, it turns out, on the knuckle of the middle finger, and across the top of the knee…)

*Does this introspecting make me more or less translucent?*

People in the neighborhood learn to keep their distance from one another, unsure of who is sick and who is not. Streets formerly bustling with mopeds and the noise of people shouting and selling chestnuts beneath lines of low-hanging laundry are now so quiet that when Q goes outside for a walk in the early evening snow there is no one even to call after her, not even about her leg. Uneasy but somewhat bemused, she goes to the corner store and buys a plunger, some first aid gauze, a dozen rolls of toilet paper, and a peach-flavored Popsicle. Then she hobbles back up to her apartment and abruptly removes her pants, dons her pink plastic slippers, and enters the flooded bathroom to take a long, milky shit.

Afterward, she removes the old bandages from her leg, and, using her thumb like a palette knife, begins the lengthy regimen of scraping the layer of thick yellow pus off the surface of her skin, reslathering it with the fresh contents of a yogurt container, and tenderly bandaging the whole thing back up again. By the time she is done with her ritual, it is nearly ten. The moon hangs sullenly out the open window.

Q looks at her face in the mirror, pressing her fingers into the soft gray sockets below her eyes. She looks like a person who spends too much time on the internet, she thinks, dipping her fingers into the nearest container and slathering the balm all over her forehead, her cheeks, her chin. She massages it in in a circular motion while clumps of cloves and chrysanthemum flowers fall into the sink and onto the flooded floor. Somewhere outside, a little dove coos. The light in the bathroom is soft and romantic.

Q applies mascara to her upper lashes and a thick pink gloss to her lips. She does this very slowly and at great excess, only stopping when her whole face appears oozing, radiant. She smacks her lips together and blinks wetly at her ethereal reflection as the moonlight sets the surface of the standing water on the floor aglow. She marvels at the roundness of the moon and the moonlike roundness of her face. Closes her eyes and feels her heavy body shimmering. *Yes, the balm is most certainly working*, she thinks, quivering.

And yet, it is not quickly absorbed. An hour passes, maybe more. Neither is she raptured nor transported. She checks her messages while she waits. Buys ten pounds of fresh persimmon online and an enormous new shoulder bag to carry them home in after. Checks her voicemail. Nothing. Nothing. Kills a mosquito by snatching it with her hand. Snaps her fingers to erase all proof. Begins plunging the shower drain.

*Does this introspecting make me more or less awake?*

Tiger visits her in her dreams. He finds his way onto her head and kneads her long hair like fresh noodles. She doesn't mind in the least that he is wild and lives in the street. Nor that he has dirty paws and fleas, or that his teeth are rotten and smell like old duck eggs. He kneads her hair, and, in this way, shows that he knows something.

"Tiger," Q whispers to him in her sleep. "Tell me how to make the most perfect balm."

The backs of her eyelids purr and paw. Everybody she's ever seen, or been. She hits restart on the dream reel using the dirty foot of her cane and watches as she walks fearlessly into the muddy river that was once a street, uprooted trees and bicycles swishing past. She watches as she reaches for the squealing box of kittens, reaching and still failing to reach them, her leg catching painfully beneath the broken debris, a slow-motion animation. She pushes each familiar slide into the distance with the tips of her eyelashes. Each familiar smell. *Go, go, gone*, she mouths, sniffing at the air.

Q knows better than to let them stay. There are things about yourself that you don't want to recognize. Pieces of the past that are more private than your private parts, even if, according to some people, you share these freely with all the internet. Some people see you, some people don't.

Other people are fleshier than they seem.

Tiger yawns and sweetly arches his back before leaving through the open window.

*Am I a poet or am I a sage? Am I superhuman or am I human? Am I a cat or am I a dog? Am I alive or am I dead?*

Write: Today I will construe myself more invisible and invincible.

Write: Today I will construe a self more beautiful than it was yesterday.

Write: To achieve this, I will conjure a gentle potion.

Write: Gentler, wilder, more or less here.

Write: Today I will endeavor to close the distance between us.

Write: Today I will work to remake myself stronger and truer.

Write: More potent than the last incarnation.

Write: If you still reject me then, then I am a truly abject person.

Write: I am not from here. I am not here.

Write: No before. No after. No more spells, just endless present logic. Where the rule is research, the art is research, the belief is research, the shelter is research…

Write: I will achieve the results I am looking for.

Write: I will obtain every kind of result.

Write: Every kind of magical thinking.

Write: Who am I if not a person brought here to problem solve?

Write: The good, the bad, the ugly, the perverse…

Write: Just because it's done in private doesn't mean it has no power.

Write: May my research take the shape of a softening fever; may it establish its own tempo, its own menace, its own cure.

Write: Better than magic, better than self-defense.

Write: Just because you can't see something doesn't mean it's not dangerous.

Write: Just because you can't see something doesn't mean it's not dangerous and there.

*What kind of research is the most mortal kind of research?*

Spring rains bring with them the usual floods. As if on cue, Q's downstairs landlady piles on to the leaking shower pipes her seasonal complaints about leaking roofs, windows, doors. And the city slowly comes back to life—albeit everyone in it, slightly changed. When Q sees the men at the bar again after many months, she barely recognizes them: they look as if they have aged a decade or more.

The cats begin coming through her window. And she feeds them—of course she does—to please nature, to please all animals, to please the mystics, to please the menace, to please the gods. Two at first, then six, then ten, their tawny stripes blending with the dappled light through the waving blinds. Q is friendly with them, even if it is true that she does not know what they get up to in the night. She is learning about and cultivating this kind of acceptance. Violences, valences. They purr and are energetic, even if their company is not the same as friendship, not the same as romantic love. They do have a certain terrible unknowability about them. Q entertains this even while, deep down, she feels fear.

## THE LONGEST WAY TO EAT A MELON

*If I blend fear and courage, will it result in a more lasting medicine?*

Things Q registers as threats, in order of perceiving them: the rusted corners of the dumpster; the street at that hour between magic hour and nightfall; the sound of a stranger's voice through the door; the foul-smelling gutter water; the foul-smelling shower water; the foul-smelling toilet bowl; the foul-smelling drain; the rising river and sinking riverbeds, their permeable outlines and borders; a feather leaving through the window; a strange feather entering through the window; the sinking flesh beneath her eye sockets, its redundant softening, blackening; thawing street ice; the men who clamor around, knowing but never quite knowing enough; the possibility of being this mortal forever; the possibility of becoming uglier and uglier with age; the texture of a cheap ointment made without the real intention to heal anything or anyone…

*If on a balmy day, a balm…*

Q wakes early one morning to the sound of yelling in the street.

She stumbles over to the window trailing bits of goo and gauze. There, the normally barren peach tree is suddenly full of blossoms; a cool breeze pushes clumps of them from side to side.

She watches as the man in the green hat tries to pry loose a city garbage can from the sidewalk. When he is unable to, he kicks it several times instead. He is barely recognizable: his hat, all dirty and ragged.

"Doesn't anybody see what she's up to?" he yells. Cab drivers pull over to the side of the road and roll down their windows to observe the unfolding action.

The man takes a handful of rocks from the ground and throws them in the direction of Q's window. The rocks fall limply from their intended course and break the window of the apartment two floors down instead. A baby inside wails.

"She's feeding them and turning them out all ruthless and fierce…" His eyes are wild and unpredictable; they roll around in their sockets like oiled marbles.

He swings at the curb for more gravel, punching violently at the gated storefronts all up and down the block as he goes. A group of shopkeepers eventually forms a circle around him and takes him down. Some rags are torn from his back. It looks as if he has been badly burned.

"Fires, thieves, ghosts," Q hears someone in the next-door window say conspiratorially, to which someone else grunts.

"*Fires, thieves, ghosts,*" Q finds herself repeating, if only to herself.

The marbles get oilier and oilier.

"I saw them going in through her window…" the man spits.

Onlookers gaze up to where he is pointing and catch Q's slippery apparition in the window frame. Her face, still moist from the previous night's ointments, appears almost entirely translucent. She does not look away.

She tries to speak, but finds her throat and tongue so parched she is unable to say anything at all.

"Oh, leave poor Q out of this," a neighbor on the floor above her says. "That's just poor Q with her bad leg…"

The man swings another handful of gravel haphazardly in Q's direction as he breaks free of the crowd and begins running toward the lower door of her building. His eyes find her in the window as he nears it, but by then Q has already turned her back.

By then Q has retreated from view and is making her way quickly to the bathroom, where she now finds herself rushing inexplicably into the flood zone, forgetting even her plastic slippers. She turns the shower tap on cold and stands there under the gushing water. She stands there in her full pajama set, not bothering to remove anything.

The water comes down, pushing the remaining ointment off her face in wide, silken sheets. The stuff collects in clumps around the wet collar of her pajama shirt and in the folded cuff of her pants, before patty-caking down onto the standing water and curdling around her ankles.

Q closes her eyes and listens to the sound of the water slapping against the pool at her feet. Listens as the kittens in the next room tumble out of her bed and pad around on the tile. There they go now, lapping at the yogurt containers and tipping over a water glass—the sound of glass shattering.

She can hear them jumping up onto her desk and padding across her computer keyboard. She can hear them jumping onto her nightstand and tearing her notebook to shreds. She thinks she can hear them helping themselves to dried scallops from the kitchen pantry, breaking all her favorite dishes, and pouring themselves bowls of milk from the fridge. Burping and clawing and pawing at the walls.

She can hear them growing larger now too. Until pretty soon the sound of their padding is replaced by a lurching. She can just make out the sound of them tearing at the curtains now—the sound of them breaking the window and punching through the walls. The sound of them pouncing out the window now. Onto the roof.

And pouncing away.
*Boom boom boom.*

## AUTOBIOGRAPHY OF A LOVER

**1**

They tell you you're too sensitive and you tell them you're not sleeping. Like, you don't lose sleep for just anyone, you know. And now you're also losing hair. You spend all day carrying others and all night vacuuming the crying-room couch.

**2**

You once told me that your hair was completely black at birth, but turned red, and then orange, and then yellow, green, blue—a new color for every person you'd loved. Now it's quite purple, and you're not even done living. Not even done dying. Not even done trying on the raw materials.

**3**

Wash your hair in the morning. Wash your hair in the evening and let it dry. Wash your hair in the afternoon…

#### 4
The nights lately are very humid, but because other people don't seem to mind, you pretend not to mind either. Air conditioners sold out for thousands of years: love letter to the makers of cross drafts.

#### 5
The worst kind of lover uses all the ice on the weekend and forgets to refill the ice cube tray.

#### 6
You make long, elaborate braids and dangle them out of the window and down over the drab city streets. People on the sidewalk duck under your waving tips, your very novel new species of tree.

#### 7
Bad witch, good witch, in-between-good-and-bad witch…

#### 8
Some people's fantasies involve sex islands, but yours is a clean kind of room enveloping whole neighborhoods.

#### 9
The sink is full of warm melodrama; the part: the wrong part for you. It's cliché to imagine why so many strands of you are always leaving—and just when the moping is getting good—

#### 10
Begin again, they tell you. They tell you you're too sensitive and so you begin again.

**11**

You get a discounted ticket and fly to a place that is lush and cool. The airplane toilets are dirty, but because other people don't seem to mind, you pretend not to mind either.

**12**

You practice using the word "lovers" crassly and sarcastically in the company of the other you.

**13**

Practice shedding tears on a good/bad game show while drinking piquette from the can and picking at a bowl of fresh olives.

**14**

Never mind about the time, or higher-order universes, or being well.

**15**

The project of spirit-interrogation that burns you turns you. You say this.

**16**

Everybody who knows anybody who gives a shit about extreme weather.

**17**

Your alibi for the week is that you're emotionally unavailable, just as moon flights go on sale for emotionally available billionaires.

**18**

The trip opens and closes without transformation.

### 19
The aisles between here and there are full of smokers.

### 20
Begin again, they tell you. They tell you you're too sensitive and so you begin again.

### 21
No point in rhyming anymore, no point in wordplay. Some friend of a friend of an old friend you knew tells you somebody who's a troubadour has a crush on you.

### 22
Something biblical about the seasons. Everyone you've ever met who has claimed to be an artist but never made a single goddamn thing.

### 23
Make that a single *visible* thing.

### 24
You have a strong urge to sleep with everyone in the city. You make copies of your apartment keys and hand them out democratically so as never to be accused of favoritism.

### 25
The hairs lost between lovers shuffle between the cushions and mix with the housebound allergens of both dog and cat.

### 26
Add up all the rainbow lockets of hair and you could weave a pretty extensive rug. Dangle it out the window and beat it with a broom.

### 27
The dust expelled from the rug is as thick as campfire smoke, the plumes exorcised from the tail as livid as your finest aesthetic categories.

### 28
Who will keep you company, you wonder, in the wildfire season?

### 29
The longest part of the day is that hour before every child on this side of the equator finally falls asleep—

### 30
Begin again, they tell you. They tell you you're too sensitive and so you begin again.

### 31
Fear of the calamity makes all your hair fall out two chapters before the end, makes kissing impossible, makes making friends feel reckless in the face of such deep weather. Fear of mounting the grassy knoll only to be met with burnt ground. Fear of consistency. Fear of the consistency of dark matter.

### 32
Because even if the purple is described as a royal purple, and the blue more ultramarine, your teenage strands of green-and-bleach-yellow gunk turn tangerine gunk red balloon just after sunset.

### 33
The loss, calculated by the equation heart minus time multiplied by the funny bone, voted on by the caring atoms.

### 34
Too much chorus for the auditorium, too much guitar pedal for the open mic. Your distrust of staying is as pronounced as your distrust of acoustic guitars.

### 35
You're so sure that the most moving part of the song is the leaving. What you call "value-added feeling." That is, until all the children wake up all at once and their wetness adds loudness to the value of crying.

### 36
Then all the songs of leaving shall be tied up with the songs about impossible gushes of cool oceanic air.

### 37
Weightless, impossible, cool, romantic, crass, sarcastic, reversible, haptic…

### 38
Love letter to the architect of departures, I see you like an X-ray into the heart of a silkworm.

### 39
Nobody told you the rehearsals would not be paid.

### 40
Begin again, they tell you. They tell you you're too sensitive and so you begin again.

### 41

Baby pulls all your hair out when you lower them into the car seat. Lover pulls all your art out when you point to the no-smoking sign.

### 42

Not all leaving is questing, but you promise it's worth it—even if just to smooth out the ragged edges.

### 43

The champagne is served in a plastic flute designed so as not to produce shards, the corners of you rounded to reduce liability.

### 44

Every travel agent in the world is now booking discount flights along the strand-paths of your romantic ideation.

### 45

"There may be fifty ways to leave your lover, but this airplane has only two," she says, walking backward down the aisle and extending both arms.

### 46

You leave by telephone. You leave by choir. You leave by serial monogamy and serial desire. You leave by polyphony. You leave by romantic attainment. You leave by gothic religiosity. You leave by classical pronouncement.

### 47

Three drinks spilled on a velveteen cushion.

**48**

Two exits by inflatable slide at each wing.

**49**

One unbearably lonesome and artless flight—

**50**

Fifty times you leave your lover until your lover's out of sight.

## OPINION GENERATOR

He had opinions, but didn't have anything to say about the project of dying or becoming. A rose is a rose is any ordinary rose, he'd say, in confidence, as if a little piece of the sun and the moon and God really was in none of us.

He had feelings, but was not sad after the Greek tragedy we saw together at the theater, or even after that real tragedy that was so devastating to the rest of us. The thunderstorm that preceded it and followed it, he said, was like a flashlight waved by an anonymous person on a faraway hill.

He had taste, but not the kind that is exercised daily in these new approaches to figurative painting. His was all about the bending into inclement weather, the daily sharpening of knife into bitter gourd. Call him an iconoclast, but he wasn't. He couldn't destroy anything with teeth or a tongue.

He knew desire, but did not make advances. Not in lively bars, not in empty ones. Nothing to do with the price of drinks.

When his friends used their elbows to egg him on, he replied only that aliens might be more open and kind, and wasn't desire just an animal with a distracting dance anyway, better reserved for the types of people whose hearts were welcome mats.

He had ambitions, but they were so slow to emerge that when they did all possible rewards had wilted in the dusk of the previous hypothermic dawn (this time, like last time, a rose).

He liked conversations that sputtered and spat up, reversed.

He liked best those aspects of the landscape that were waterlogged and transitional.

He liked prose poetry and the never-ending middles of weeks, and so much so, that when one day he put a loonie into the meter to pay for extra time, the machine gave him a prescription for another kind of universe.

## ELEMENTARY BRIOCHE

### Chapter 1. Where Has Tian Fang Gone

Tian Fang was just sixteen when he went to the Big City. He packed some clothes, his watercolor brushes and paints, and got on a bus one day that was blue with an orange stripe, or else it was orange with a green stripe, he can't remember, and after a couple of hours he got off the bus again and was a stranger in a place.

The city was not at all how he expected it would be. Instead of tall buildings, there were elevators with glass balls on the tops that you could ride to if you had money. If you didn't have money though, and most people did not, well then you could just stay at the bottom and live under a tree, which is what he did from Day One to Day Twenty, painting portraits of passersby for small coins.

He never told anyone back home where he was going or that he was even planning to go. Many years later, decades even, he liked to imagine they might still be wondering. Had he married someone on the other side of the ocean? Had he been struck by lightning in a field? Had he committed some kind of crime, bought a motorcycle, and disappeared into the mountains? Where had Tian Fang gone?

The truth is though that nobody wondered. In those days, nobody ever wondered where anyone else had gone because it was obvious when someone left that they had just gone to the Big City.

On Day Twenty-One, Tian Fang suspended his plan to paint for a living and got a job cutting hair at a salon at the university, moving into a bunk bed on campus. He cut hair there twelve hours a day, and for the remaining twelve hours he could be found either eating noodles at the canteen, reading magazines in his bunk, or sleeping. He still didn't know how he'd gotten that job, given that prior to that he'd never even held an electric razor. *Someone must have been in a good mood that day and decided to give a stranger a chance*, he thought. *People did that sometimes*, he thought. *Gave others a chance*, he thought.

The students whose hair he cut complained endlessly. About their heavy course loads, about the air pollution, about their lack of parental funds. About the smudges on their glasses, and the greasiness of the food. About the slowness of food-delivery apps, delivering drink after drink full of melted ice cubes, and the trouble with people who came to the Big City only to eat brioche every day and never learn the fucking language.

All the while, Tian Fang just nodded. He thought it strange that no one ever complained to him about the haircuts he gave, even though he was quite sure they were very bad. He approached each job as he would any other artwork, fashioning on each student's head the figure of a brave young bird breaking free from its mother's nest. Restless, tangled, full of potential. Students, it seemed, knew a great deal about many things, but did not have this kind of basic orientation toward action.

**Chapter 2. I've Been Here for More Than Two Months**

*Complements of duration are used to express the duration of an action or a state.*

*Subject + Verb + Complement of Duration*

(1) ~~She at university has studied for two years.~~
Soon Tian Fang can tell everyone he's lived in the city for <u>two months</u>.

(2) ~~He in China lived for one year.~~
Never mind that Tian Fang every night reads magazines for <u>two hours</u> and checks his phone for <u>three</u>.

(3) ~~I every day exercise for one hour.~~
He figures he will be working <u>two hundred years</u> to save up the kind of money he needs to live (and I mean *really* live) in the Big City.

(4) ~~He went swimming~~ swam ~~one afternoon.~~
While he knows not what to expect of the <u>X number of years</u> otherwise known as the future, he imagines that it will be as beautiful as the best watercolor paintings, washing over him as gentle, undulating color and light.

(5) ~~She studied new words~~ studied ~~for more than~~ <u>two months</u>.
Tian Fang watches videos <u>every couple of hours for a couple of minutes</u> on how to confidently trim hair with a razor.

(6) ~~We here wait for her for a while.~~
He has never but might otherwise have enjoyed <u>every day all day</u> eating expensive imported brioche in his pajamas.

### Chapter 3. She Came Right After Breakfast

Mary had loved Tian Fang from the very first moment they met. From the very first moment she'd lowered herself into that squeaky salon chair and felt the swoosh of air over her lap as he came in with the plastic cape...from the moment he fastened the cape around her neck and toggled the chair up and down...from the moment he touched her temples to adjust the angle of her head...

Well!

Mary felt as if her heart might burst.

Mary had come to the Big City with a dream just like everybody else. And just like everybody else, she'd been surprised to learn when she arrived that she would not be invited to live in one of those big shiny glass balls in the sky. Mary got a job cleaning the elevators that took others up to the sky instead, a job she disliked. It wasn't long before she began to organize her discontents.

Her shift started at five in the morning, after the ravers got home, and ended around noon. She spent most of her time mopping up vomit from the elevator's marble floor, unplugging crunched beer cans from the ceiling air vent, and scrubbing makeup stains off the walls. She often wondered what people had been up to in there, but knew better than to ask. Instead, she swallowed off-label ginger capsules before and after each shift because the smell and the motion of the elevators made her sick, and because it was her goal to work quickly under these conditions. The quicker she completed her daily duties, she knew, the quicker she could also retreat to the stairwell, where she and her fellow workers kept stashed a curated selection of anarchic zines and labor bulletins. She learned a lot from these materials. It now seemed remarkable to her, for instance, that the world could be organized the way it was. It seemed to her that change would be simple and inevitable, and that it was right around the corner.

The only thing that Mary did genuinely enjoy about her time in the elevators: the sound of the looping classical piano music that tinkled like stardust inside, reminding her of her childhood dream to one day be a great composer.

"What'll it be?" Tian Fang asked, fluffing her hair. It was unclear whether or not he remembered her, though she'd been to the salon now several times. He seemed more distracted than usual.

"Just a little trim..." she started shyly, as Tian Fang began snipping away. Really she'd meant to show him the magazine cutout she'd brought with her in her purse—an otherworldly image of a transcendental punk singer with cropped black hair and raccoon-like eyeliner—but instead, Mary just sat there, blushing and submissive, his scissors flitting about her like paper fans. After a whole shift worked in the elevators, it was often difficult to conjure words. At least, this was the story she kept telling herself, her excuse for being such a quote, unquote kitchen slipper. And what was this terrible music they were playing?

Tian Fang looked impatiently from the clock to the mirror to the back of her head. Asked her what she had been up to that day.

"I came right after breakfast," Mary croaked. Truthfully, she'd just gotten off work, and had eaten half a coconut bun on her way over. It was one in the afternoon.

"You know, you look a little bit like this artist I used to know," Tian Fang said in a faraway voice.

"Oh yeah?" Mary's heart raced. She observed her pale reflection in the mirror, her hair all limp and wet, one side slightly longer than the other. Well, she thought, she certainly would have *liked* to be an artist. Yes, wouldn't that have been nice!

"You wouldn't know them though," Tian Fang added. "They weren't famous or anything."

"Oh…"

"Not in the least."

Mary looked at the ground.

"Just someone I sort of knew. Actually, I heard they recently died."

**Chapter 4. Rock, Scissors, Cloth**

"So what do you do for a living?" Tian Fang asked, after a pause.

"I'm a composer," Mary found herself saying, growing ever pinker as the words left her mouth.

"Ha, ha, ha. Me too."

"Really," she persisted. "I live at the top of one of the elevators."

Tian Fang smirked.

"You don't look like the glass-ball type," he said.

"No?" She took a breath. "That may be true..."

What was she getting herself into now!

"...But I won the keys in a game of rock, scissors, cloth."

Tian Fang dropped his scissors and fumbled around on the floor to retrieve them. When he rose again, he looked visibly flustered.

"Impossible..." he muttered.

"Not impossible," Mary said, matter-of-factly. "When you think about it, the odds are fairly good..."

The way Tian Fang was holding the scissors now—timidly, and with both hands—made him look like an adorable baby emperor. He looked like an adorable, bewildered baby emperor. *It was impossible what she was saying*, he thought. *Absolutely impossible*. Then again: if moving to the Big City didn't make impossible things possible, what would have been the point of moving to the Big City?

"Not impossible," Mary said again, as if reading his mind. She made a playful little rock with her fist and pretended to bash the scissors from his hands.

**Chapter 5. I Like Music More Than You Do**

*The comparative sentence is used to show the difference between two persons or things.*

A "compared to" B + Adjective

(1) ~~Planes compared to cars are faster.~~
Mary <u>compared to</u> Tian Fang is <u>more cunning</u> on account of her years-longer spent in the Big City.

(2) ~~Watermelons compared to apples are bigger.~~
She schemes even while Tian Fang, <u>compared to</u> Mary, busies himself <u>trying to gain the upper hand</u>.

(3) ~~Elephants compared to pandas are heavier.~~
Mary <u>compared to</u> Tian Fang is <u>more habituated</u> to the surreality of the social ladder (elevator) and therefore sees through its indecent conglomerations of status and power toward the possibility of other, brighter futures.

## JACQUELYN ZONG-LI ROSS

*A "compared to" B + Verb + Object/Complement of State*

(1) ~~You compared to him like learning new words more.~~
Certainly, Mary <u>compared to</u> Tian Fang eats shrimp <u>less</u>. It's expensive, after all—the good kind, the right kind—and she is determined not to let material excesses like shrimp or taste obscure her noble plans for the revolution.

(2) ~~She compared to me likes music more.~~
Mary <u>compared to</u> Tian Fang likes music <u>more</u>. Even if she doesn't yet have the money to buy a proper piano, her dreams are filled with its imaginary and very tender notes. She will play it, her piano, after the revolution. She tells herself this daily.

(3) ~~I compared to you tested on the exam better.~~
Mary <u>compared to</u> Tian Fang knows <u>more than</u> she admits she knows. She knows, for instance, how to leverage her invisible labor to wreak havoc on the system, how to boycott and how to divest, how to organize a union, and even how to build a Molotov cocktail, though she hopes never to use one.

*The negative form of "compared to" is "do not have," not "not than."*

(1) ~~Panda <u>does not have</u> elephant <u>as heavy</u>.~~
Tian Fang <u>does not</u> <u>have</u> Mary <u>as complete</u> a vision.

(2) ~~Elephant <u>does not have</u> panda <u>as love of bamboo</u>.~~
Mary <u>does not</u> <u>have</u> Tian Fang <u>as much patience</u> for bureaucratic systems.

(3) ~~Bamboo <u>does not have</u> panda <u>as love of bamboo</u>.~~
While both struggle with ideas of justice and merit, Mary <u>does not</u> <u>have</u> Tian Fang <u>as outlandish a sense of utopian possibility</u>...(See next.)

**Chapter 6. So You Like Her Style**

Now *of course* Tian Fang was in love with someone else (what kind of story would this be otherwise?) and from Day Twenty-Nine to Day Eighty-Five, all Tian Fang could think was, *If only I and the beautiful gallerist from Elevator Six Hundred and Sixty-Three could just meet one day and go riding the elevators up and down, surely she would give me a show, and this whole thing about moving to the Big City at the tender age of sixteen just to work for very poor money without any weekends or holidays would be well worth it in the end and I would be very grateful for having come.*

### Chapter 7. Your Name's Great

Tian Fang blasted Mary with the blow-dryer and chattered excitedly to her about his fantasy encounter with the beautiful gallerist. He would show her the biggest paintings first, of course, before bringing out the smaller, weirder pieces. He showed Mary some photos of the gallery and the beautiful gallerist on his phone. What a spectacular view of the Big City they would have up there! If only she would recognize his talent in a city as big as theirs!

What was it like living at the top of one of those elevators, he wanted to know. Did Mary have a gym in her building, did she have a pool? Could she watch the sun setting every evening from her bath or bed? And how was it, really, still finding the time and energy to compose music, in the midst of so much beauty and comfort?

But Mary wasn't listening. She was too busy staring out the window, a feeling of heartbreak invisibly filling her up like tap water into a solid-colored water bottle. The feeling started in the hollows of her feet and moved up her legs, filling the cavern of her torso, until eventually the feeling reached her neck and threatened to flow over.

"What's your name again?" Tian Fang finally asked as Mary screwed on the lid, just tightly enough to prevent emotional seepage, but loosely enough to produce human sound.

"Mary," she croaked. "My name's Mary."

"That's a great name, Mary," Tian Fang said, dusting the split ends from her cloak as she slumped from the chair to the counter to pay her bill.

### Chapter 8. Mary Cried

Mary went directly from the salon with her bad haircut and heartbreak to her patch of grass under a tree and promptly started to cry. There she cried for three days and three nights under the protection of a very large leaf and, on the fourth day, stubbornly removed the leaf and went out into the world.

Things appeared brighter out there than they had been before. The glass buildings sparkled like the teeth of celebrities, and the river sparkled like celebrity teeth too. Polluted fish flipped belly up on the surface, but that part was just fine. The world was good.

Mary even showed up to work four days late and wasn't fired, since no one was around to fire her. Her coworker just kind of shrugged when she arrived and handed Mary a spray bottle, passing with it a small, folded note into her concealed palm.

Someone had roped off one of the vomit-encrusted elevators in her absence to keep it from being used, while in the other, the beer cans had simply been kicked out into the lobby to make room for the riders. The piano track skipped on a trilling high C, but she didn't have the care or authority to fix it. How long might this have gone on, she wondered, had she decided never to return? Would the good people of the Big City simply allow their home to decline into a permanent wasteland?

**Chapter 9. The Bus Is Starting Up, So Let's Hurry**

*The verbs "come" and "go" are used after some verbs to function as complements of direction. "Come" is used to indicate an action occurring toward the speaker/thing being referred to, and "go" is used to indicate an action occurring away from the speaker/thing being referred to.*

*Verb + Object + Complement of Direction ("come"/"go")*

(1) ~~She from Taiwan has~~ <u>returned come</u>?
Mary no longer remembers how long she's <u>been in came</u> to the Big City. Most people in it don't because time in there <u>moves goes</u> differently.

(2) ~~Teacher Lin at the classroom waits for you.~~ <u>Hurry up go.</u>
She thinks, *I probably just came to have my heart broken*, and, with the passing of time, eventually <u>starts comes</u> to believe it.

(3) ~~Mary returned to the dorm went to eat toast.~~
Mary <u>returns</u> to the tree <u>goes</u> and unfolds the note, makes arrangements to attend the after-hours workers' meeting.

(4) ~~Teacher Lin already by car came.~~
Saves her money to <u>buy</u> buns from the good bakery <u>go</u>, not the bad one.

(5) ~~He just last week back to America went.~~
Seasons <u>come and come and come</u> and <u>go</u>.

(6) ~~If you return to the school come, just give me a call.~~
(Remember: if you <u>stay</u> long enough <u>come</u>, your failures in the city may only be further compounded.)

(7) ~~She likes when arriving in my kitchen come to with me chat.~~
If both Mary and Tian Fang really do <u>believe</u> in destiny, why not in a kitchen just <u>come</u> together and conspire toward a more surprising ending?

(8) ~~Bring her some little melon when you go, okay?~~
This <u>coming</u> together <u>going</u> would be good for the story.

## Chapter 10. The Winter in His Hometown Is as Cold as in Beijing

Meanwhile, winter was now upon them, and the city no longer resembled the city of opportunity that Tian Fang had first come to inhabit.

The snow that lay over the Big City transformed it from a lively, vibrant place into an oppressively gray one. The white stuff covered up all the things about it that he had liked best: the food stalls, the bicycles, the girls in miniskirts. Now all the people of the Big City were bundled up in the most distasteful fashions: toques and scarves and heavy-soled boots, plasticized black puffer coats draping from the tops of their heads all the way to their ankles. The people of the Big City now resembled a factory of drying sausages, all bunched up and linked together at bus stops and around the entrances to escalators. Within a matter of weeks, the merely gray had transformed into a hopeless gray sludge. And the worst part about it all was that Tian Fang recognized this sludge instantly.

## THE LONGEST WAY TO EAT A MELON

It reminded him of his hometown.

Tian Fang finished his shift at the salon and went around to the back of the building where there were a few rusty lawn chairs, a rusty picnic table, and a rusty old bucket all spread out in the parking lot. Tian Fang made himself a fire in the bucket and sat down in the nearest chair. Got out his sketchbook and began to draw. It was negative twenty-something Celsius out, but the heater in his room had been broken for weeks. A pigeon bobbed out of the bushes and cooed. At the other end of the lane, a large crowd was slowly assembling with handmade banners and signs.

Suppose he quit his job at the salon, he thought. What then? A young man like him who was just setting out on his own for the first time had no real skills, besides those forged in the service of his artistic calling. Leaving the salon now would also mean he'd have to give up his bunk at the university, and maybe even go back to living under a tree. This prospect wouldn't have bothered him so much had it been the middle of summer, but it was not the middle of summer anymore.

Returning to his hometown, on the other hand, had always been out of the question, as doing so would only concretize his failure. The last thing he wanted was to have to make up some elaborate story about his adventures in the Big City, only to have to make up an even more elaborate story about his reasons for leaving it.

Tian Fang watched in silence as the procession of workers moved down the alleyway and rounded the corner onto the university boulevard, their eyes and mouths alight with a restless sadness and fury. Their chants faded just as quickly as they had arrived, the evening traffic soon recommencing behind them.

*If not art, what is the point of all this living, striving?* Tian Fang thought. *What is the point of all this pain?*

### Chapter 11. Did You Find My Passport

Now imagine: finding a golden ticket on the floor of an elevator. Imagine it: a golden key. Or imagine it's a passport, someone's wallet, even—doesn't matter. The point is the same. Imagine finding something on the floor of an elevator that gives a person from the underworld access to an elaborate upper world. Some place where artworks are suspended in beautiful glass balls.

Is it stealing if you don't stand to benefit? Or if whatever is gained was, in fact, owed? If you destroy an object merely on principle and eat only stale coconut buns afterward just as you have always done...if your impatience with an unjust system results in some kind of eruption, some kind of outburst, but hurts no one...is it such a crime? To wish for an abstract revenge? What is the role of the arts in these kinds of situations?

**Chapter 12. What Is She Doing**

Mary took the elevator back down to the ground, ran all the way to the canal, and threw the gallerist's passport into the dirty yellow water.

**Chapter 12½. What Is She Doing (Part Two)**

The foreign passport was later retrieved downstream by a fisherman, who took it home and handed it to his wife, who left it on the counter to dry and later be found by their daughter, who put it in her schoolbag with every intention of illegally selling it, but who got scared and instead dropped it off in a hurry at the salon on her way to class at the university.

Lucky things do sometimes happen in the Big City. (Or what would be the point of living in the Big City?)

## Chapter 13. I Got Them All Correct

*The verbs "finish," "understand," "see"/"hear," "open," "up," "to," "give," "become" and the adjectives "good," "agree," "wrong," "familiar," "early," "late," etcetera can be placed after a verb to indicate the result of the action.*

*Affirmative form: Verb + Complement of Result*

(1) ~~I listened understood what the teacher said.~~
Tian Fang should have known that the universe would always <u>conspire become</u> against him.

(2) ~~I looked saw Mary at the sport court doing tai chi.~~
Mary too <u>believed agreed</u> that luck would only get people like her so far.

(3) ~~Today's homework I did finish.~~
It's entirely possible that the whole concept of <u>finding seeing</u> one's soulmate does not in fact make for a compelling narrative.

*Negative form: "Do not have" + Verb + Complement of Result*

(1) ~~You didn't listen hear what he said?~~
It <u>wasn't</u> so much about <u>loving opening</u> as it was about <u>openly loving, caring</u>.

(2) ~~These clothes have not washed finished.~~
Upholding a version of the Big City as being <u>not</u> <u>dirty and wrong</u> but <u>open and good</u> and <u>good and open</u> should be the goal of any young person coming to the Big City.

(3) ~~I have not looked seen your dictionary.~~
I <u>don't</u> like much to <u>read early</u> anyway. (We don't have any more patience for your fancy fucking brioche.)

**Chapter 14. Happy Birthday to You**

Tian Fang was not at work the day the gallerist showed up to retrieve her passport, though he was the first to hear about it afterward.

Having been cajoled into a haircut by an overconfident stylist who'd tried to leverage the return for some basic social media influence, she'd finally left in a fury, threatening a century of wigs and hats, her hair permed to the texture of dragon's beard floss.

Tian Fang nearly wept when he heard about it the next day. On Day One Hundred and Forty-Nine in the Big City, he simply could not believe his bad luck. What a day he'd picked to take a day off! His birthday, no less! The only day off he'd had all month! What a day he'd picked to be born!

Tian Fang left the salon and took the subway downtown, where he spent a good part of that tragic day-after-his-birthday skulking tearfully around the entrance to Elevator Six Hundred and Sixty-Three, plying for a way to get into the building. The Big City was a hoax, a money-suck, a dirty black hole. It was nothing at all like he'd been promised, and nothing had gone as planned, not a single thing, since the day he arrived. He finally wished he'd never come.

When eventually he was able to sneak in by following a food-delivery guy through the front doors and into the elevator, he began to panic. He looked himself up and down in the mirrored elevator interior: he looked like he'd been up all night crying (he had); his hair was greasy, his T-shirt crumpled and stained. What was it that he had even wanted to say to the beautiful gallerist?

The two began riding the elevator up in the direction of the penthouse, both Tian Fang and the delivery guy politely looking at their shoes. The sound of classical piano music tinkled like stardust inside.

Tian Fang closed his eyes.

Tian Fang closed his eyes and was immediately transported to his grandparents' house in their hometown: to afternoons spent there as a child dozing on their stiffly upholstered settee and listening to classical records on their dusty turntable, the one with the bent needle. *Tha-dump, tha-dump, tha-dump.* He smelled the inviting fragrance of warm buns baking in the oven, felt the warm beam of sunlight on his face through the open window. Outside, children were screaming and riding bikes.

*Where had Tian Fang gone?*

He opened his eyes as the elevator jolted to a stop at the penultimate floor, sending the elevator cab swinging. The piano music cut and the lights went out.

"Are we going to die?" the delivery guy asked in a whisper. There were mysterious banging sounds coming from the elevator shaft above them. A faint smell of smoke.

"I don't know," Tian Fang replied in the dark. He was still thinking about his hometown, alternating waves of nausea and nostalgia washing over him in beats.

"I wasn't even going to take this run," the delivery guy complained, "but decided to at the last minute. Now imagine, if this was the end…"

Tian Fang listened as the stranger slid down to the floor and began uncrunching the top of the paper bag he was holding. Tian Fang listened as the delivery guy took a long sip from a drink and unwrapped some kind of sandwich.

Tian Fang slumped to the floor opposite him and began to cry. For himself. For others.

He cried and cried. And cried and cried and cried.

Three minutes later, the lights came back on and the elevator slammed upward toward the penthouse with a screech.

## Chapter 15. The Sunset in the City Is as Beautiful as It Is Everywhere Else

Tian Fang stumbled out into the empty gallery and squinted as streaks of orange and pink streamed in through the windows, illuminating the space like a morning-after dance floor. The whole place had been ransacked; a smoky haze hung over the top half of the room like a cloud. The window coverings had been torched and torn down from their brackets, and there was broken glass all over the floor. There were small craters on the walls where paintings had once hung.

Now Tian Fang *could* have tried to piece together exactly what had happened, *could* have tried to alert someone, to call security... but no.

In that moment, all Tian Fang could think about was his own damn bad luck.

For the first time since moving to the Big City—on Day One Hundred and Fifty, and not one day more, not one day less—Tian Fang began to wonder whether bad luck really was a part of living in the Big City, or whether bad luck was merely a part of being him.

### Chapter 16. Meet You Where the Sky Meets the Sea

Tian Fang walked to the window and looked out over the city. It was the first time he'd ever seen the view from a glass ball in the sky. And it was just as beautiful as he'd always imagined.

A fire alarm began to sound, but Tian Fang did not hear it. He did not budge. Behind him, the doors of the elevator closed and the elevator began its slow descent back to ground.

Tian Fang stood there, transfixed, in the glow of the orange-pink sunset, watching calmly as small passenger boats crisscrossed the glittering canal below. It seemed impossible to him that the city could be so big, and he so very, very small, and that all of them just went along with this scheme, fitting together in whatever way they could. How was anyone supposed to find anyone in such a place? How was anyone supposed to find themselves?

Mary arrived and grabbed hold of his hand, leading him out of the smoky gallery and down into the emergency stairwell. It was only when they were about halfway down—down fifty flights, or more—that Tian Fang suddenly became alert to the sound of the piano track skipping loudly on a trilling high C and the sensation of descending, Mary's warm hand in his. Down and down and down they went, until finally they reached the bottom and ran out of the building. Out into the cool evening air.

### Chapter 17. A Homecoming

The light in the streets had tipped from orange to pink to a brilliant electric purple, and every shadow in their path now tilted and waved with a drunken, erotic current.

Mary and Tian Fang held hands in the dusk and ran excitedly through the crowds, while all around them, people fought and danced and laughed and cried holding their children and their elders and their comrades and their lovers. The city's mounting symphonic soundtrack blared triumphantly from an elsewhere-loudspeaker—at once everywhere and ostensibly nowhere at all—emptying the heroic streets of their burgeoning subplots and minor characters.

They passed through the belly of a marching band and curbs filled with protesters and beguiled tourists. Ran down alleys of lively street vendors and food kiosks and roving dogs and rats. They ran through the sprinklers of the French quarter leaving handprints on all the windows and depressions in all the hedges;

ran through a fluorescent supermall full of spinning signs and mascots, catching noodles on their tongues. They ran down into the subway system, hopping over turnstiles and laughing through the jaws of narrowly closing subway cars, and danced over heaps of discarded rental bikes and the hoods of moving taxis.

Riding a plastic swan, they moved softly around the circumference of a candlelit pond awash with bobbing water lilies. They watched melancholically as night-flight floatplanes took off over the distant harbor.

The music got louder and louder as they went, only quieting again as they approached the canal.

By then it was almost morning.

## Chapter 18. Have You Heard the Piano Concerto Yellow River

Mary sat down next to Tian Fang on the grass and offered him half of the coconut bun she had packed in her bag, unfolding it gently from a piece of frayed fabric. Her face, he only now noticed in the approaching dawn, was covered in black soot, like she'd been in some kind of explosion.

"I cut it myself, if you're wondering," she said, referring to her charred hair, which she now fluffed around her ears. "I didn't like what you'd done with it last time. Too long at the back, and the bangs—well. It was a bad haircut. You give really terrible haircuts..."

Mary shoved the half coconut bun into her mouth and slowly began to chew.

"...But don't worry. This city's full of them. Good cuts and bad cuts. Good moments and bad moments. Good people and bad people... Most probably couldn't win a game of rock, scissors, cloth if they tried." Mary swallowed forcefully.

"Too hot in summer, too cold in winter..."

Her stomach emitted a chorus of unsettling sounds.

"I'm thinking of leaving, by the way," she told him. "Have you ever heard the piano concerto *Yellow River*? I'm thinking of taking it. The river, I mean. And taking it inland this time, instead of outward toward the sea. You can come if you want..."

*But what's wrong with the Big City...* Tian Fang caught himself thinking as he rotated the cold half bun in his hands 360 degrees. This time though, Tian Fang needed no reply.

They watched as a passing crane dropped a huge shit into the canal. The shit floated on the polluted surface of the water for a while, forming a ring of scum around it, before eventually sinking.

## TWELVE FORECASTS

### 1

Now through next Friday, your superficial struggle for recognition obscures the quest. A conversation you have with an old friend will remind you of why you do what you do and refresh your creative direction. Beware of self-doubt, but be comfortable using ultramarine blue, at least until Neptune completes its rotation on the twelfth of February.

### 2

As Pluto moves into its ninth orbit around the sun, creative spirits are high. Keep impulses in check by remaining steadfast in your search for a more elegant solution, however understated. True progress is often quiet rather than prolific. Potential avenues for research may include: children's blocks, perennial gardens, systems of non-English phonemes... Note the importance of exterior, interior, and spiritual structures, and take great care in the kinds of shelters you build.

### 3

Resourcefulness is the name of the game this month, Virgo. Limit your writing surfaces to scraps of paper: prescriptions, napkins, used bus tickets. Do not inflate the importance of writing. Instead, consider new possibilities for economy in all aspects; be flexible, and alert to flourishes. Think of William Carlos Williams, who managed to fix broken arms while also giving people something to read in the waiting room. Be deliberate about the projects and small luxuries you choose to retain.

### 4

Thursday shapes up to be all about process. You might spill coffee on a stranger, drop your phone in a public toilet, or drive away with an important package on the roof of your car. Sometimes there's nothing left to do but paint looping, lopsided watercolor Os on the wrong kind of paper and occasionally rest your head on the table to sigh. But try embracing disheveled hair, and turn it into something that appears intentional. Be at peace with the simple gesture of placing your waterlogged phone in a bag of rice—doing so without expectations.

### 5

Recall that December studio visit with the curator of seriousness. "It's all part of a professional practice," she told you. Attending artist talks: "a practice." Reading poetry: "a practice." Talking to people on the phone, going for drinks... "all part of a professional practice." You may have been frightened at first by the adultness of the idea—preferring to noodle around on the guitar into the late morning without calling it anything at all—but the approaching solar eclipse marks a transition in your thinking. So take new pleasure in the practice of sending lengthy emails to prospective employers without punctuation, or paying twelve dollars a day for the luxury of writing in a loud café rather than in your living room. If looking like shit is important to you, at least try to consider it a practice and do it every day. Consistency is key.

### 6

Embrace the ambiguity of fact and fiction this month as Saturn's rings drift an eighth of a degree. Give yourself permission to wander and to imagine different, and alternate, futures. Assemble long paper chains of consequential and inconsequential thinking; fill your pockets with the holy symbolism of bear-shaped stones and shards of sea glass. Feel the borders of yourself dissolving and merging with the weather, with your protagonist, their moods and imperfections. The strength of the story can be weighed in the things that you find and the histories that you invent for them.

### 7

Transiting Taurus manifests as a blank page this Monday, leaving you listless and disillusioned. Rather than force it, wait for inspiration to arrive in the dust slowly collecting on your pen. If you look very closely for a week or more, you will become a better reader of Proust. Liken your talents to a million tiny particles and have faith that their expressions will soon fall into place.

### 8

This Sunday, sincerity rules. Hold in your mind that highest image of romance: of magic-hour gazebos and regal elderly couples sashaying lustily beneath them. Take a risk, and trust your own brave public gestures. Cheek to cheek, gold teeth gleaming... If you forget the choreography, learn to improvise.

## 9

As Leo rises over the eastern horizon, the dormant quadrants of your studio leaf out wispily and wirily and all on their own. Pictures you haven't seen in years, now with wants and needs and no boundaries. But try exercising looseness rather than restraint. Cast off your painting smock and let down your hair! Let a charcoal line be your cattle path, and linseed oil your desert moonlight. Nearing the end of March, Venus will deliver an unexpected reward for your careful abandon.

## 10

The stars realign this week, bringing misunderstanding for Gemini. Rather than seek clarity, try abstraction on for size. Reconceive of your wardrobe as wearable sculpture. Learn to move and talk and eat and sleep in shades of mauve, with no more than a vague feeling about it. Record from a great distance the atmospheric pressure building in the wider language until just the right kind of language coagulates. Then spill it forth from your whole person, without being representational about the spilling.

## 11

Attention comes in abundance this month. There's a boy in the bookstore who spies on you relentlessly through the shelves as you browse the used-poetry section, and another one who winks when you ask for a lemon-poppyseed scone. Wednesday confirms the coolness of your intellectual charm when you are complimented by an admirer with a PhD on your off-the-cuff application of Deleuze and the Pink Panther ("…imitates nothing…paints the world…pink on pink…"). Be wary of these distractions, lest you miss your true love on the street. Also note that it can be harder to make art when you share a bed.

## 12

Fear not metanarrative, for it is on your side. From smallness comes precision, and from precision comes humility. Between now and next Thursday, work on crafting a detailed description of the view from your window. Consider the implications of the landscape, the sloping cars and buildings and straggly margins of grasses. Consider the secret lives that populate its alleyways and the contexts for their quiet movements. Consider relative warmth, and relative cold. Consider your own sensations of numbness. What is trueness, exactitude. Sometime soon, these details will move you.

## BRAIN, NO BRAIN

I go to the mall with my hair wet and the lady at the lotto counter tells me it's very bad luck. What part of it's bad though I don't ask, don't care. I choose numbers at random. I pay with change. I've always curtsied through the winter air. Never owned a hair dryer.

She pushes a shiny ticket toward me and her eyes in the mirrored surface aren't even superstitious. They follow me anyway. Some people are just like that. Two blocks east to a scrubby park and a bench with defensively designed armrests still slippery with bottles from Saturday. I sit down and scratch away all nine horseshoes on my Beginner's Luck, hoping for three matching numbers and ten thousand dollars. I know my chances are bad, something like one in twelve million, but I don't mind. I want to turn off my brain.

Brain says, "Focus." Brain tells me to be more deliberate, more clear.

No Brain bats her lashes and blinks, blinks and fixes her sloppy ponytail.

"Writing should be organic, a channeling of truth," Brain says. "So write, or don't write, but *don't just try.*"

No Brain shudders, takes a slow sip of zucchi— I mean, *cucumber* water from her glass. She is thinking Courgette. Summer Squash. Spaghettini in the cupboard. Daylight Savings. Socks.

She puts her drink down on the mantle and goes idly to the closet to get out the vacuum. She plugs the cord into the wall and begins noisily vacuuming the hall.

"Stop it!" Brain cries. "I can't think with that thing on!" But No Brain is busy, busy singing now too.

Brain collapses on the sofa, her sore head throbbing, and curses into the pillow that is not a pillow but a mountain of hard books on deceptively soft topics like performance and phenomenology and the politics of feelings. She squints at the elusive quote by Merleau-Ponty positioned cruelly below her eyeballs. "The body is our general medium for having a world," it says.

On the internet I read that snails have a circuit of just two neurons in the brain that are responsible for decision-making: one that establishes the presence of food, and another that establishes the presence of hunger. I look closely at the elaborate illustration of a snail's physiology in my browser window. "Despite being poor sighted and entirely deaf," the article reads, "snails are gifted in associative thinking. They make connections between things without drawing on logic or past experience."

I close my laptop and walk in three tight circles around the neighborhood. Toss my contact lenses in a trash bin after the first lap, and stuff dirty napkins in my ears after the second. Without sight or sound, the third lap is endless and experienced as great swaths of color. As fear and unbearable brightness. As the shudder of a hammer drill and the chilliness of rain and the gravity of heavy creatures moving swiftly toward me and away from me. Ask how much longer I could go on like this, in the school of sensing and feeling, and the answer is not long: just because you like the way being present *looks* and *sounds* doesn't mean it works for you. Imagine, forever, moving like that, all snapped open, with your heart on the ground.

Food and hunger, but what about danger?

I pretend to have experiences, but privately experience only threats.

Someone behind a cedar hedge once told me there was a magic portal behind the shrubbery, but all I found there was a dirty puddle (the only proof of the puddle's portaldom was that it was warm). Don't worry though, I'm the opposite of naive. Not defenseless either. My armor is the equivalent of a meter-thick shell. I move swiftly in the opposite direction of danger, ten thousand times quicker than a snail. Rather, the slowest parts of me are the insides. Those spare, empathizing neurons. I have an intense desire to see secret things explicitly, to understand how the personal connects to many other millions of kinds of personal. Who knows what kind of trouble I could be in next for even disclosing these vulnerabilities.

The laps continue over the course of an hour and I grow famished, thirsty, frail. I fall to the sidewalk doing my best impression of a pained martyr, audience zero, eyeballs bulging while clutching my gut. I make my body as low and horizontal as possible, as dejected and trample-able as possible, as I press the flats of my hands against the wet cement, the flat of my cheek, the flat of my belly, in order to maximize my public contact with hardness. I only move when a passing stranger politely asks me to—and even then, I make sure to do so sorely and reluctantly—transferring my body weight section by section, intention by intention, from toe to throat to fingertip. I clear the sidewalk and move spinelessly in the direction of the nearest blackberry bush as raging squirrels approach my bloodied body from all sides. There, among the rattiest of grasses, I find myself shoving one, then two, then three spiny branches into my mouth. Thorns and all. A dog pisses beside me but I do not stop, not even to breathe normally. I gulp at the air. I know very well how my lolling around both helps and harms others.

The writing for me comes easiest when I am sober. Because sobriety is more inexplicable than drunkenness when it comes right down to it. And because I am searching for this quality in my writing.

Brain fumbles with the pen, fumbles with the keyboard. Tendinitis in my thumbs and forefingers from other kinds of existing. *Too much doing makes the thinking parts suffer*, Brain thinks. *Too much doing necessitates technologies like dictation into thin air*, which she refuses.

A sudden itch in my mouse-clicking finger travels up my forearm and into my shoulder, sending my whole arm spasming. Suddenly the itch has swept everything from my desk onto the floor. This surprises me and angers me. Then, as if on cue, I feel a creeping delight.

I retrieve a vintage electronic keyboard from the closet and dust it off, tenderly placing it atop my desk. Plug it in and turn it on. Sternly select from the list of demo tracks unlocked via a yellow button. Then I awkwardly begin to dance.

Out the window, an unexpected windstorm. Brain dances as the clamor of branches ignite in the street—timidly at first, and then with more weight. She dances until the angles of her limbs match the clamor of the branches. Until the crisscrossing of the car headlights match the angles of her limbs. Until the cratered surface of the moon appears magnified in their headlights. She dances until she appears quite electrified in the window.

Brain dances and dances and cannot stop.

"Some people engage in risky activities because it is their method of forgetting," a therapist tells me, the day after the day I buy another losing lottery ticket that, while not in itself a risky activity so much as a long shot, nonetheless symbolizes the same fatalist approach to life and life purpose that tends to be viewed by others in this universe of hard work = sane work = positive capability as *a liability*. I wonder about that "forgetting" part too: how the word hangs like a tail between the legs, presuming some obvious, shared loss of innocence. Her suggestion that I have pieces of myself I'm trying to forget irks me. Like she's got her finger inside of me and is feeling around for more guts. I refuse to let her at them. I refuse to be soft. What kind of medicine could be more effective than a No-Brain Brain?

In the end though, the exhilaration I glean from withholding only deepens the self-sabotage. Wanting time and time again to take more time than I should with the things that for others appear to take nothing. This, among the list of activities that are riskiest to the memorizing lobes and cortices. This, among the invisible sequences of decisions that render one unreliable, undesirable, unpredictable, unforgivable.

She encourages me to try something called the "think-aloud

protocol" to take stock of my impulses as they are occurring. "A kind of performative self-talk," she says. "And no, I *don't* mean the crazy kind," winking.

"But I might say things I regret," I warn. "I might say things that are not at all what I mean. I might say things that I do mean, all mixed up with the things that I don't. Until all the things that mean something will be indistinguishable from the things that mean nothing…"

She keeps her hands confidently folded in her lap to communicate patience and control. I pretend not to notice when she inexplicably breaks out into laughter then, turning my head to instead take in the details of my surroundings: the stuffy room with the window that remains closed to keep out the noise of the train; the ugly microfiber couch with its compressed middle cushion; the scattered cow-print pillows; the pitcher of water and two empty glasses, poised. *The very opposite of the kinds of details that can angle a person toward eureka*, I think. I rewind my body to the point in the movie when I still believe it might be possible anyway, just to be a good sport, right—like maybe she needs me more than the other way around.

I take off my sweater then put it back on, inside out, and bike quickly away in more unpredictable weather.

"A monkey's wedding!" someone calls from a passing car, meaning: sunny and rainy at the same time.


Write in the morning and feel you have all day, write at night and feel you're already late. Late to the project that is supposedly all of you, which means that you're late to being you too. Late to being you. Imagine. There is no middle day for art. I walk all over the place, unbelievably, and still rarely have a good idea.

## THE LONGEST WAY TO EAT A MELON

To consider the activity of writing is to choose between two possible outpourings: the first being totally vulnerable, bare, and the second being vulnerable but only insofar as to expose certain parts. A question of selection and self-preservation then, a series of choices between you and you. Followed by the writing getting writing, followed by the writing finding its spine, followed by the writing getting done, line by line. *And where's the art in that?* the nonmakers say. *Where's the brain? The hardness, the madness...*

Around this time in the evening, the moron doesn't know when to quit. And the nut, the obsédé, only wants to wake from the same dream. Over and over. Only wants to walk the same route. Until eventually something is arrived at by sheer force. By now it's midnight. The moron stops talking. But the stylist, whose pockets are full of such variously shaped rocks, can't stop touching them until three a.m. The critic breaks it all down for us in the morning. Into brains and not...

I can continue this way for quite a while, in spite of my body breaking down.

(Later, thinking out loud in the clutter of an intersection in which two cars collide a few feet from where I would have been if I'd decided *not* to jaywalk: the probability that my thinking aloud has manifested disaster *versus* the happenstance of impulsive events still saving and saving my life...)

Brain goes to the mall to buy a new pair of sunglasses for the vacation she promises herself she will take.

She imagines what it will be like to be on vacation. What it will be like to eat nothing but junk, read nothing but junk, watch nothing but junk, think nothing. Clouds shaped like baby animals without the capacity to defend themselves. Clouds shaped like a pantry full of pickles that will last all winter. Clouds shaped like first aid kits and earthquake kits, just in case, like sunblock against all possible melanoma.

She imagines building a sandcastle without the consultation of architects or engineers, without worrying about density or ephemerality, even though they are endemic to the form. She imagines sitting on a wet towel under the sun and the sky and enjoying their basic complementary relationship without being troubled by the unoriginality of this thinking (or worse, the possibility of becoming herself basic in the process). She rehearses the conversation she will have with a friend on the phone after being away for what feels like a long, long while, now a seasoned traveler who knows how to laugh about losing her passport, mobile phone, and wallet all at the same time. *How lucky I am to have landed in the only hotel without cockroaches! How freeing it is to call you on a pay phone with the foreign coins I just so happened to find jingling around in my pocket!*

What kind of sunglasses even suit a brain?

At the end of all the imagining she worries there will be nothing left to do but go.


On thinking and remembering: throw a trail of treats down on the ground in the direction you want to go.

On thinking and maximums: okay now to place those littlest of details in the donation bin.

On thinking and paralysis: forget the thought that pains you.

On thinking and psychosis: forget the pets and people that distract you.

# THE LONGEST WAY TO EAT A MELON

    On thinking in the landscape: more a mood than a place you drive to.
    On thinking with suitcase in hand: full of waterlogged tools.
    On thinking in a backward time: fancy, like the interior of a novel.
    On thinking and taking the garbage out: still once a week.
    On thinking from a burned-out shed: zen-like if you let it be.
    On thinking and poetry: cliché until that one time a hammer.
    On thinking with rhythm: through the body of a snail.
    On thinking in okay condition: less productive than you realize.


I'm taking the garbage out now—the garbage, and the compost, and the recycling—in bags and buckets and boxes in my arms. Out the door and down the hall, the weight of the living in my wrists. Down two flights of stairs with the empty shells of the stuff I consumed yesterday tossed together with the day and the days before that. No need to elaborate. Exactly and always already all the things you imagine.

I'm opening the back door with my elbow now. Now I'm outside. Standing in the alley in the randomized rain. Alone with myself and the shells of the stuff of myself. I throw the garbage into the dumpster and begin emptying the rest into a line of bins. The plastic, the glass, the paper recycling. Alone with the probability of being no one. The glass bottles smash into pieces when I throw them down.

I'm thinking about all the work I have to do. Organized from A to Z plus some ecstatic punctuation. All the visible and invisible work. About the disappointment of not doing it, and the disappointing absence of sex if I do. All the laundering and psychic laundering and hammering and psychic hammering. Tonight, before I fall asleep. All the drawing and redrawing.

I'm emptying the compost pail now. Whole pieces of the world, wasted. An orange rind sticks to the bottom of the bucket and can't be shaken out. No such thing as an original thought.


No Brain is whistling, whistling as she walks. No Brain is having a field day.

She looks at a tree being choked by a chain-link fence and experiences the glorious absence of thought, follows the fence down to the place where it hits dirt and experiences the same. Behind her, Brain follows grudgingly, picking up all the articles of clothing that she's tossed off. A shawl, a sweater, a wide-brimmed hat, a blazer, a bra, a bangle, a belt...

A giant sinkhole opens up in the street and, not thinking, No Brain walks directly into it.

"Help me!" she screams, from the bottom of the hole, waist-deep in sewage and slimy stink. Tampons and surgical gloves float by her in clumps as a flustered Brain tries frantically to recall what exactly it was she was taught in her emergency-response training. (Was it first call for help, or open the airway? Fire, police, paramedic?) She eventually lowers one end of the belt into the hole and hoists a sopping No Brain up.

"I-I-I *saved your life*," Brain stutters, shaken by the frailty of existence, as the crowd of onlookers claps and then abruptly disperses, unchanged.

But No Brain is already back on her feet, and whistling, whistling, whistling as she walks. She looks like a bog queen but she doesn't care. She just smiles in her winning way and carries on.


It was like the day I caught a piece of pineapple in the air and experienced for the first time how wet pineapple really is, how unexpectedly rubbery and wet. Really, I should have thrown it right back, but no. Instead, I chose peace: placing the chunk of fruit between my lips and humming into it, sending the sour yellow shape vibrating down my spine while I mumbled things to my insides like, "You're stupid," and, "You're sexy," and, "You're possibly allergic."

I imagine the window blowing open and the train horn filling my ears. The middle cushion exploding, the Kleenex catching fire. I imagine the pitcher of water shattering and flooding the room. The tumultuous weather. Reactions are nonintellectual. The worst part about it. I imagine her kissing me. I imagine her slapping me across the face. I imagine the worst part about it being the feeling of no obligation. The confusion, the betrayal, the hangover, the goodness—

I try to imagine a single, messy, unassuming event that might force my body and brain into alignment.


No Brain wants to know what Brain most deeply desires.

"What I desire?" Brain laughs. "What I want most of all is to relinquish control."

"I want it to rain, or not rain."

"I want to scream, to be fucked."

"I want to be given lots of money, or none at all."

"I want to be institutionalized."

"I want to be famished in a hospital, or well fed in a prison."

"I want all the channels to be selected for me so that all I have to do is switch things on or off."

"I want to hand over my fate to a lucky number, a lucky charm."

"I want to be submissive if it means I can be unaware of my own submission."

"I want to be an automatic writer."

"An automatic playlist."

"An automatic window."

"An automatic car."

"I want to be a snail, a slug, a single-celled organism."

"I want to be a fish out of water on the concrete banks of a suburban creek."

"I want to be so hot I bubble over and so cold my limbs fall off."

"I want to be a girl, just a girl, with a room full of tidy objects."

"I want to sell everything, or lose everything, or have nothing to sell."

"I want to state my cause because my cause is poor."

"I want you to twist my arm and make me lose big money."

"I want to believe that each person is either one hundred percent virtuous or pure evil."

"I want to believe each person."

"I want to expect nothing of our millionaires, or our billionaires, or our homeless."

"I want all the superfluous details to wash over me and make me float."

"I want to be an absolutely shameless kind of tourist."

"The worst kind of fan."

"I want to be thrown from a window like a grand piano still playing 'Heart and Soul.'"

"I want to believe in any kind of art, any kind at all, or no kind."

"I want to peel myself off the pavement like a cartoon roadrunner."

"I want to use everything exactly once and never think another thing about it."

"I want to be forced to eat expired meat until my migraines expire."

"I want to move from this rock to that rock using only my fists."

"I want to exit the internet via a horrible book."

"I want to lose myself in the loudest television."

"I want to be painted as a kitten with a very common name."

"I want to be painted as a kitten with three legs and a mane."

"I want to be blown like a naked kite."

"I want to be written off as an idiot, or a complete genius."

"I want to feel as if the brain is an inside-out sweater."

"A compressed middle cushion."

"An exploding middle cushion."

"I want to be laid like a daisy in a public path."

"I want to be left on the curb with my bad decisions."

"I want to be symptomatic in my reasoning about the past and future."

"I want to be present tense filled with no choice in the matter."

"I want to move chaotically in the opposite direction of the sun."

"I want to be sworn at in languages postgrammar."

"I want to return and find everything exactly as I left it."

"I want to return to lick the boot of my manager."

"I want the impossible, plus the possible, in this universe."

"I want not love but a reason to pass."

"I want to prepare for no more than two types of weather."

"I want to live in a house with a diamond-encrusted toilet."

"I want to be draped in magazines printed on the wrong kind of paper."

"I want to breathe in the fumes of the new highway expansion."

"I want to know my own phone as possessed by abstract buttons."

"I want to jump into the air and experience no landing."

"I want to get on a bus to a nowhere town with a supermall."

"I want to marry young there and settle down in that town."

"I want to lie down like an egg in the middle of the parking lot, frying."

"And bear children to a stranger there without expectation."

"Without a Brain, and a No Brain, to keep me company."

"Without the particles of dread so clearly formed in my head."

"Without a compelling reason to intellectualize anything."

"Or else I want to remove my head instead."

## THE LONGEST WAY TO EAT A MELON

I hold it quite happily in my arms: this melon that I have spent my whole life tending. It is round and full of potential. Bulging with ego and grandiose expectations.

Sometimes though, when I am feeling not quite like myself, I find myself hiding it under a bed, or swathing it in some stiff canvas that I have recently stripped from a failed painting. I don't know why I do this—only that the point of the exercise is not to think too much.

There's a little bridge outside my house that crosses a ravine, and some days I am tempted to throw the thing overboard.

"How else can I be expected to carry it home?" I ask my mom. "It's so heavy I feel like a prisoner towing one of those big metal balls. How am I supposed to feel inspired under these kinds of conditions?" She tells me not to worry too much. "Quick, put it in this string bag, then hang it from your elbow and don't think any more about it."

And so I go to a friend's house using the amnesiac string-bag method, and when I arrive, my friend greets me on the threshold with a chisel and a wooden spoon. She has dust all over her face and looks like I imagine Rodin might have looked when he was busy making *The Thinker*. She invites me in, and we eat some peanuts together at the kitchen counter, scraping the shells off onto the floor, basically daring each other to do so, until the whole performance begins to feel too obscene and my friend is compelled to get a dustpan. She sweeps the floor briskly before heading out the screen door to sprinkle the shells into the nearest garden bed. I follow her out with my handful of peanuts, half hoping she'll ask me about the thing that I have brought, but she does not. Everything out there is dead or dying.

"I think I finally figured out what the problem is," my friend puffs. She adjusts the nozzle on a tangled green hose and begins blasting narrow holes into the dirt at close range, holding the hose against her hip like a limp bazooka. Soon the small planter is flooded, transformed into a sinister black pool, more a crystal ball than a place for growing things. "*Irrigation…*" she is saying, over and over again, as earthworms come floating to the surface. It's been an unusually scorching summer, and things aren't growing like they used to. I worry that my friend will come to resent me.

We go back inside together and, because I can't put it off any longer, I pick up the string bag and roll its contents out onto the table. We both stare at it for a while in silence, afraid to get too close. My friend finally extends a hand and sets it gently wobbling across the surface. It has a strange way of moving, like a raw egg that all of a sudden changes its mind halfway through and decides to act like a hard-boiled one. "Huh," she says. Then, after a while: "I'll admit I've never seen one quite like this before." She sends it wobbling again, this time much more aggressively, while loose strands of hair shake from her head and fall all over the table.

"Me neither," I say. "But I need to make the most of it, somehow."

My friend backs up a few steps and examines it from a distance, tilting her head to one side and crossing her arms over her chest. She has a troubled look on her face, a look I've only ever seen when she is reading something disturbing in the newspaper.

"I think you'd better use a solid utensil," she says finally. "And be as decisive as possible. Don't let the process drag on too long." She looks at me as I pull a long strand of hair off my bottom lip.

"You're right," I say, flicking it into the air. "Thank you."

Another moment passes.

"And what would you consider to be too long?" I ask.

"Hard to say. Some people seem to make the most of things right away, while still others can take months, even years…"

I nod heavily. A ladybug has followed me into the kitchen and is now on the move down the length of my arm. I gently remove it and place it on board a deserted peanut shell.

"Why don't you take these," my friend says, brightening, as she abruptly hands me her chisel and her wooden spoon. "I'm done in the studio today. You can return them later."

I take the utensils from her, examining each like the fine bow of a violin.

"Okay," I say, rolling up the tools in a clean paper napkin, and placing everything in my saggy string bag. Then I lace up my shoes and head home.

It used to strike me as impressive to have something to tend to so carefully. I used to see other, older people carrying theirs around in the street and think that it must be some kind of proof of their good character to have grown something so wholesome and robust—an A grade, a medal, a sticker, a star. But no, I now know that there are no rules as to how one can be grown, or what one chooses to make of it afterward: only that some people will be tormented by the process, while others will be emboldened by it.

"What would you do if you had one?" friends ask each other over impassioned drinks on weekends. "What kind of statement would you make if you had such a fantastic opportunity?"

"I'd do something avant-garde," one person says. "*Experimental.*"

"I'd make something for the greater good," someone else says, bowing under the table to blow their nose.

"Whatever I made, I'd want it to be absolutely singular," says another with a boastful tone. "And to taste not at all like you'd expect…"

Others murmur their accord.

"I'd want to share mine with as many people as possible," someone whispers.

"No, no, no," says another. "It would be much wiser to keep it for yourself. To make it last a long time."

"…and to make a crunching sound when you cut into it, like the sound of a car being impounded," the boastful person continues.

"I'd want to make something very delicate, as thin as tissue paper," someone with a mousy voice says. "To reduce it to a shimmering substance…"

"And what about you?" someone finally asks. "What do you plan to do with yours?"

The little hairs on my arms stand up. My feet rest limply on the bundle under the barstool.

"I don't… I don't *know* exactly…"

"Come on, you must have some idea?"

"No, I…" I look at the wall for inspiration. A stilted clock hand jolts aggressively forward and backward.

"I really haven't the slightest idea." My circle of friends lean in closer. "Like, I used to *want* to make something remarkable too—really, I did, in art school, you know, before I had a melon of my own. But now that I have one, well...I feel as if every *molecule* of my making brain has been...has been, ummm...*obliterated*...I mean, has been *obliterated* by an *enormous*, a GINORMOUS...ummmmm..."

No one dares take a sip of their drink. Even the people at the neighboring tables have turned around to listen. But for the goofy plonking of the rain hitting a metal dog dish through a broken windowpane, the mood is palpably somber.

"What I mean to say is: you stare at something for long enough in the dark and pretty soon the thing begins to lose its shape. Begins to lose its color, its structure, its smell. Not *literally*, but *philosophically*, you know?"

My friends are quite sorry to have asked.

At home, I lay the melon down very gently on my desk alongside the chisel and the wooden spoon. Then I leave the room and have a long, hot shower. I put some music on, and make a nice dinner. I do all the dishes, even the pots and pans. I open the windows. All of this to put myself in the right state of mind.

When it comes right down to it though, I am again intimidated beyond belief. We are equal and oppositely attracted opponents. It seems preposterous to me that I, a flawed human being, could ever make something more wonderful than a melon in its natural state. I pick up the wooden spoon and use the back side to tap the hard of it in the round. I feel awkwardly as if I am going to bed with someone for the first time, laughing nervously while trying to appear desirable. The spoon makes a slapping, puddingy sound.

I put down the spoon and send a message to a stranger on the internet.

"How would you approach the task?" I ask, followed by a string of alien emojis.

A few seconds pass and then a waving ellipsis appears.

"It very much depends on which planet you're from," the stranger replies. Then, after a pause: "Or which planet you're heading to next."

I close the tab and message another stranger on the internet.

"I'm feeling vulnerable," I say. "This latest project has really got me in shackles."

"Really," the stranger writes. "That's hot. You should come over."

"I'm not kidding. I feel genuinely unwell."

"You're making me thirsty."

"I've got to make the most of this, and soon. Before it's too late."

"I don't even care what you mean. Come over?"

The stranger sends me a photo, but I close the tab before the image loads.

I work hard each day to learn how to sling it. I work hard each day to improve my swing. And because I'm not one hundred percent sure whether my therapist told me to *sling* it or *swing* it, I just work hard on both in the hopes of gaining some kind of practical advantage over the object that has been causing me so much grief. I keep the heat turned down real low in my apartment to quicken my creative process, and, surprisingly, it does. Soon friends I pass on the street are telling me how good I am looking lately. How confident, how self-assured. "You must really be making the most if it," they say, through puritanical smiles. "*We can't wait to see what you do.*"

In my hours of procrastination I find myself using the chisel to whittle down the wooden spoon until it comes to resemble a totally average toothpick. The melon remains intact.

"Couldn't you have just gone out and bought a toothpick from a store," my friend later whines, "rather than ruin my one good spoon?" I tell her not to worry about the spoon. What's important is that, in all matters of slinging and swinging, a person take an utterly original approach. "And original approaches take up valuable time and resources," I say. She sighs reluctantly in agreement.

I cross and cross and cross the ravine, each day becoming a little bit stronger and more used to the feeling.


In matters of etiquette, it is important to consult a trusted source. I call up my dad and ask him how best to begin.

"Diagonally," he says, without hesitation, as if this is the most obvious answer.

I call up my aunt and she agrees. "Yes, you must absolutely begin a melon diagonally."

I thank them both for their advice, but once again, that evening, cannot figure out how to do as they say. If the diagonal is achieved too quickly, the result will be perceived as clumsy or craftless; if I proceed too slowly, one risks a deathly literalness. Why can nothing these days be straightforward?

I lie in bed in my fleece pajamas, nesting the elusive fruit between my knees.

What if I crack it open too early, before it has reached the height of its sweetness? What if, when I do, it doesn't taste like I imagine? What if I wait so long that it begins to rot? Or if, totally unbeknownst to me, its insides are already rotten?

These are the kinds of things that keep me up at night. The kinds of things that make me want to throw up every fruit I have ever eaten.

I roll the thing up in its canvas swaddling and toss it frustratedly under the bed. It makes a little thud and cracks gently open when it hits the wall, but because I am already sleeping, I do not hear it.

# THE BREATH OF HAN & HAN

### The Year Was 1901 and It Was the Age of Breath.
### The Age of Breath and Han & Han.

Two identical twins gifted with supernatural synchronicity were accidentally separated at birth and accidentally given the same name at opposite ends of the Earth. There each lived for many years, aware of neither a sibling nor a superpower.

—Now what exactly do you mean by a "supernatural synchronicity"?

—I mean, when one breathed in, the other breathed out.

—Huh.

—Reciprocal puffs of air—

—There's a term for that, I'm sure of it, somewhere in the dictionary of saxophones...

—Strangers only to themselves—

—Circular breathing?

—No: *reciprocally*, a bellows.

—And what happens when one of them dies?
—Oh, don't worry about that yet.
—What was it like then, before either one of them was born?
—The important thing to know is that it was the Age of Breath.
—*The Age of Breath and Han & Han.*

**Han Lived in the Icy Little Town of _____**

and liked singing in the shower and planting potatoes in the snow. There was never such an all-around pleasant person as Han or someone with a more easygoing temperament, especially for somewhere so cold. Han was gentle and hopeful, an animal lover and a community-garden volunteer. Han had more friends than you could count, meaning whenever you had a problem, there was always Han you could call on. Han would bring everyone seed potatoes in the spring and help them plant them, so that, in the fall, the town's cellars would be full of potatoes. Han made the rounds with an antique brass watering can that tinkled when it was filled, and made the occasional sound too when it sat empty.[1] Freezing and thawing and freezing and thawing. Nobody dared tell Han just how often it happened that the potatoes Han planted developed hollow hearts.

---

1 *Ping, ping, ping.*

**The Other Han Lived in the Dusty Little Town of _____**

and worked as a barkeep at a saloon. The saloon was very hot; the roof sloped like a reed against the midday sun. All the men inside carried loaded pistols. Still, the place was the real heart of the community—the saloon doors always swinging open and closed—and Han got on well enough with the customers, even if this Han, like the other Han, was actually a bit of a softy. Han's softness meant that, just one night a week, the saloon was given permission to transform into a kind of philosophers' café, with ideas nights, slam-poetry nights, open mics, and so on. Han came to life at these events, serving up homemade chili and Han's famous fries and fluttering all around to keep everyone's pint glasses foaming. The rest of the week, Han sat quietly behind the bar counter whittling souvenir knickknacks for tourists using a small pocketknife gifted to Han by Han's mother. The knife made a satisfying sound when it hit wood.[2] A sound like a knuckle against millennia-old bamboo.

---

2 *Chock, chock, chock, chock.*

### You Can Imagine It Now, Can't You?

—Two parallel streams of air.
—Two parallel resonances, two parallel rooms.
—Blowing, buzzing, swooshing, shushing…
—Making the whole world giddy with its exhalations.
—Because there's breathing, then there's really breathing (in and out, out and in)…
—With the *whole* heart, the *whole* mind, the *whole* soul—
—Except you mean the whole *diaphragm* now, don't you? You don't really mean the soul…
—You're right. I mean the whole diaphragm, which most of us use wrong.
—It's easy to do, use the diaphragm wrong—
—Don't you mean it's easy to use right? It's so easy it hurts. Here's how to do it:

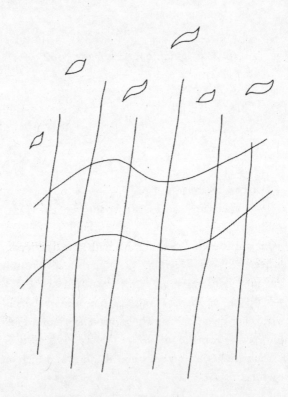

(birds rustling through far-up bamboo)

*Ping, Ping, Ping*

was the kind of music Han came from, after all: delicate, birdlike, and metallic. It was the kind of sound best complemented by earth notes: wood blocks, potato blocks, and the knocking of a knuckle against far-up bamboo.

Han moved through the pristine snow of the town, watering everything along the way with precious breath and melted glaciers. Looking for potatoes and other potato-shaped bells. Stomping and stamping. Replenishing with spare rain. *Ping, ping, ping, ping.* Freezing and thawing and thawing and freezing.

**The Music of Han's *Chock Chock Chock*ing**

meanwhile lit up the air with the dullest but most electric earth notes, beckoning to the other Han from Han's great distance without either Han even being conscious of it doing so.

*Here at last,* thought the Breath of Han & Han. *Here at last are the familiar kinds of notes composed by familiar birds and transposed by familiar boars and made loud by the most familiar rain and melted glaciers.*

Scraping and thumping and thumping and scraping.

*Chock, chock, chock, chock.*

### Now Imagine These Additional Details:

The rhythm of the breath, moving speech, but not just speech [3]
The rhythm of it, moving whole bodies too
Announcing each billowing *chin* and each *trail* [4]
The moon, the moon, open face of a clarinet player—
Or was it an accordion player: her rounded palms
Pressurizing whole alphabets. [5] Whole syllables, lungs
What looked, from space, like a giant accordion [6]
Sucking, ringing, kinking, swaying
Thinking, [7] dancing, clicking, quaking
The favorite subject matter of poets, painters, musicians [8]

---

3 Beginning with the vowels *A, E, I, O, U*…
4 The suction of air preceding someone's arrival, and the gust of air trailing after them in their wake.
5 *B, P, M, F*…
6 Wavy as eelgrass.
7 Beats per thought (bpt).
8 (Their goodness, their flatness, their holeness, their fullness.)

What lovers made love to when they weren't thinking only of themselves
Puffing and puffing to amass a supernatural dent [9]
A dent in the Breath of Han & Han. [10]

---

[9] In the cheek.
[10] (When one breathes in, the other breathes out.)

### "A Wind Instrument Is a Musical Instrument

that contains some type of resonator (usually a tube) in which a column of air is set into vibration by the player blowing into (or over) a mouthpiece set at or near the end of the resonator. The pitch of the vibration is determined by the length of the tube and by manual modifications of the effective length of the vibrating column of air. In the case of some wind instruments, sound is produced by blowing through a reed; others require buzzing into a metal mouthpiece; while yet others require the player to blow into a hole at an edge, which splits the air column and creates the sound."

**Diagram of a Saxophone Breathing Circularly**

**Or Make It Reciprocally, a Bellows**

## Blowing, Buzzing

**Opening, Resonator, Bell**

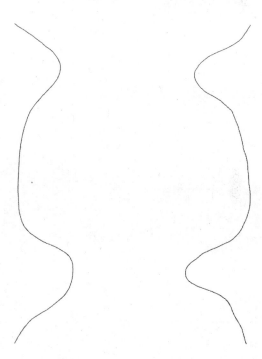

**One Winter Night, the Icy Little Town of _____**

experienced a mighty blizzard, the likes of which its residents had never known. The snow blew in in droves, ripping whole trees out of the ground, before covering their uprooted sideways bodies in ice so thick that their woody debris could not be differentiated from the hills and the community gardens and the cottages with people stranded inside of them. The few residents who would survive the night would do so by lying very still in a warm pocket of breath until they could be dug out in the morning. For the first time in a long time, life, from the surface, became indistinguishable from nonlife.

Han's potatoes were blown right out of their beds, swirled around in the air, and discarded into the sea. The few tubers that did remain were buried deep, deep in the snow and later dug up by packs of roving wolves and carried far, far away to feed their hungry litters... all this, in dens too deep to find and too dark to ever awaken from.

Still, strong-lunged Han survived the night in a pocket of breath and, when morning came, stumbled out of the snowbank to dig out the neighbors.

The very next day, the roof of Han's own house fell in, but no one came to return the favor.

The breath of the world funneled through the town, pointing like an arrow over the hills. Eventually Han packed up a rucksack of essentials and followed it. Clear, clear. Clear out of town. No destination in sight at all…and nothing but a sleeping bag, a hammer, a pot. Oh, and a watering can—a sentimental thing, really. Something for spirit, as they say. *Ping, ping, ping.* Should, by chance, one not return.

**Meanwhile, in the Dusty Little Town of _____**

a frozen potato hit the window of the saloon and broke it. Funny the things that will happen when you're pining to make something happen.

It was late morning and some of the regulars from the philosophers' café had pushed a couple of tables together under the window to converse. They chewed cold fries with open mouths and spat them out onto the floor between sentences.

"...But the best part *about* the breath is that it's circular," someone was saying, a saxophone player. "Blowing and buzzing and holding in the cheeks...When one half fills, the other empties..."

The saxophone player got up onto the table and blew a narrow channel of air full of imagined shapes and sounds up into the light fixture. Everyone clapped when the saxophone player returned to the stool.

"But nobody knows how long an age will last—only that it will go on and on and on until one day, it is no longer," someone interjected.

"You're right," said another. "What will you do after the Age of Breath? You get by now, but how will you get by then?"

The potato arrived through the window, sending shards of glass sprinkling all around like free jazz before landing in the farthest beer glass. A brave little ball of foam leaped up onto the saxophone player's flared left nostril. Everyone went quiet. Then they started to laugh.

Han came over to the table and plucked the tuber from the beer, holding it, dripping, up to the light. It was rough and gray and rather odd in shape: round but a bit elongated, with bite marks down one side.

"A meteor, right?" someone finally said. "I've never seen one, but I always thought, when I did, that it'd be some kind of sign…"

**Try to Imagine It in the Diaphragm:**

An obstruction, the size of a potato, in the bellows. Modifying and making rotten the column of air. Rattling it, shuffling it, pickling it, clogging it. Introducing conflict in the resonant chamber.

    —*But no no no, not conflict!*
    —Oh, okay. *Movement.*
    —I didn't know this was supposed to be a dance…
    —*Music*, then. Just think of it as music. Take, for example, the sound of a blizzard blowing…
    (*imitates the sound of a blizzard*)
    Or the sound of sleeping animals…
    (*imitates the sound of animals breathing*)
    The sound of a watering can…
    (*ping, ping, ping*)
    Or the sound of a knife against a block of wood…
    (_____)

Blowing one half into the other half...
(*imitates the sound of two halves colliding*)
The out into the in, and the in into the out...
(*creeeeeeeeeeeeeeeeeeeeeeeeEEEEEk*)
From one town to the other town...
(*swish swish swash*)

From one Han to the other Han, soundlessly traversing the resonant chamber...

**...Later That Night**

whittling a flute from the hollow heart of a potato that had blown, just that day, from the icy little town of _____ into the dusty little town of _____, blowing, against all odds, across the most impressive psychogeographical distances, to land, but not only to land—to transform!—like a scrawny polar larva into the most frighteningly eyed desert moth—into a musical instrument of such remarkable and unexpected beauty, such perfectly imperfect, moving, resonant pitch...

...There, on the front porch of the saloon in that most unusual wind, Han wondered for the first time in Han's life about Han's own parents: where they came from, where they might be now.

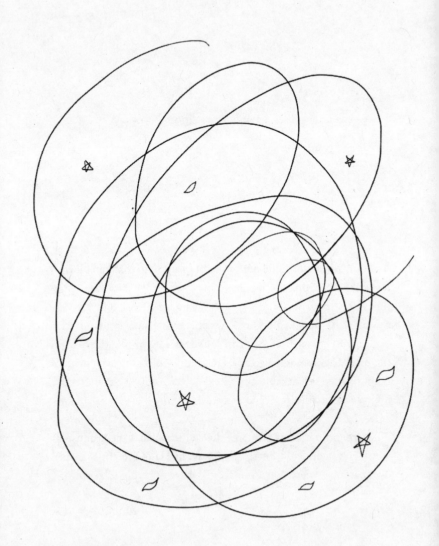

**Diagram of a Remarkable Sound Traveling Across Land**

**Diagram of a Remarkable Sound Traveling Across Water**

**Diagram of a Remarkable Sound Entering the Ear Canal**

### And Altering, Permanently, the Heart[11]

---

11 The heart, the heart, hollow heart of an accordion—

## "A _____ Is a _____

that contains some type of _____ (usually a _____) in which a _____ is set into vibration by the player blowing into (or over) a _____ set at or near the end of the _____. The _____ of the vibration is determined by the length of the _____ and by manual modifications of the effective length of the vibrating _____. In the case of some _____, sound is produced by blowing through a _____; others require buzzing into a _____; while yet others require the player to blow into a _____ at an edge, which splits the _____ and creates the sound."

**Alto Range**

## Alto Range, Tenor Range

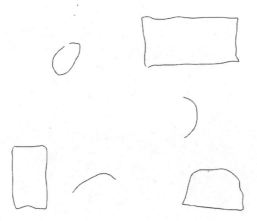

**Alto Range, Tenor Range, Bass Range**

(When one breathed in, the other breathed out.)

**Consider, for a Moment, the Magical Properties of Magnets.**

Of positive and negative charges. Of pulling together and forcing apart. Consider the frightening force of their separation, the fiendishness of their attraction, the snapping together.

Now consider the immensity of that charge held in tension by the thinnest, most invisible thread—the thinnest, most invisible thread running the circumference of the Earth—what is miles and miles and miles—what is kilometers and kilometers *of pure, golden bells*—and note all the life that that kind of thread might be making possible, you know, by *sheer energetic thread*—sounding everything you love, have ever loved—all that wind, hill, sky—and you might begin, just *begin* to imagine the kind of fear the universe must have felt that fated day that was the birth of Han & Han. Just to bother with such a precarious kind of banishment, you know. To opposite ends of the Earth, no less. And then to craft this most childlike scheme of ice and dust and breath and noise and expect it to hold everything in suspension forever...

...*Good luck!* I would have told the universe. *Good luck with that!*

**But *What If***

Han & Han were too similar to each other, too similar in charge? *What if* they were not so much yin & yang as yin & yin or yang & yang? *What if* the doubleness of their meeting—the doubling up, doubling over, by and by—the sheer excess of breath and breathlessness—might not in fact do the universe any kind of good,[12] but, on the contrary, usher in some kind of exponentially[13] catastrophic disaster, the likes of which humankind had never known?

The very possibility of Han & Han ever meeting ushered in a feathery, out-of-body fear: not gloomy so much as so high-pitched it was impossible to hear clearly. Spent fear, spent mood, spent dread. That feeling of holding your breath in the final minute before Y2K—that feeling of being completely in the dark.

How would it end? How would it begin?

---

12  In the manner of $1 + 1 = 2, 2 + 2 = 4, 4 + 4 = 8\ldots$
13  In the manner of $2^2 = 4, 2^3 = 8, 2^4 = 16, 2^5 = 32\ldots$

**Han Listened**

as Han's flute song carried, swanlike, through the air and eventually planted itself, swan-shit-like, in the canal of Han's ear, before traveling, downward, downward, downward, past the eardrum and into the sinuses, down the throat in the heavy direction of the heart, where the sound that sounded at first like a flute melded slowly into an alto, and then a tenor, and then a baritone saxophone, and the sound that sounded from thereon rather like a saxophone became, by way of a single valve—in the reluctant movement between the bottom-left and -right ventricles—as heavy and soulful as the bellow of a bandonion.[14]

---

14  How much time passes in the lonely ventricle? In that space without clocks, without watches, and without batteries?

**Han Wandered in the Lonely Direction of the Sound**

thinking, all the while, not about the breath at all, and certainly not about inhaling or exhaling in supernatural synchronicity, but instead, about Han's unfortunate tendency, since childhood, to ruin any and all remarkable encounters. Whatever it was, Han would find a way. Han moved against this inevitability in the simple manner of wading into the ocean: displacing a little volume of water with each forward motion even while feeling, with each step, that the next one might prove disastrous.

The only sounds in the world then were the sounds of Han's watering can—half empty, *ping*ing, sloshing over the hills—and the sounds of the other Han's loneliest of flute songs: what might as well be described as the loneliest songs in all the world.

(People told them their journeying had nothing at all
to do with longing

but in the end it had everything to do with longing.)

### The Music Grew Louder and Louder

until it became almost unbearable. A loudness like the most unbelievable traffic. Or like a student symphony—an entire high school band—hired by a performance artist to interrupt the traffic of one's thinking. Honking, clapping, chirping, terrible... *crescendo*!

Han & Han's synchronized breaths quickened and the breath of the world quickened with them, the time between each inhale and exhale gradually shortening to the length of a single saxophone note. Soon the charge of Han & Han's ever-closening proximity was quite literally felt in the lungs, and there they were, breathing in and out, out and in, in and out, so close, so very close, geographically speaking, that by now they were basically doing CPR on each other, geographically speaking, but also symphonically speaking, harmonically speaking, claustrophobically speaking... The sonic effect of their proximity was that of a lonely bird pecking relentlessly against the ice contained in the hollow of a frozen watering can. *Be free! Be free! Be free! Be free!*

**As It Happened**

Han & Han had now landed, in their soundings, mere kilometers from each other, with nothing more than a little hill barely ten meters high to obstruct each other's view.

**Han Had Built a Little House of Sticks**

and learned to harvest wild potatoes in the snow. Han had even become quite fond of the routine: scavenging for tubers and grubs each morning, showering below a suspended watering can slung over a tree branch each afternoon, and making small fires for cooking at night. When Han breathed in, all the little birds in the trees rustled with birdsong. When Han breathed out, the fire swelled.

**The Other Han Lived on the Other Side of the Hill**

on the bank of a river, having set out one night from the dusty little town of _____ while sounding a potato in the starlight.

What had been intended as a short night stroll had been transposed, inexplicably, into a chorus of no return.

Han spent mornings exploring the hillside and afternoons whittling away a makeshift bar counter out of a well-placed tree stump. Han stayed up late wandering the slope and inventing new flute songs before falling asleep haphazardly at a slightly different angle each night, belly up on the bare earth, flute tucked warmly under one armpit.

**Han & Han Might Have Lived This Way**

for all of eternity, had it not been for what happened next. Alas, the positions of the magnets could not be fixed: the time had come for the forces of destiny to overtake the anxieties of the universe...

...and one day, the top of the hill merely exploded.

### You Have the Most Incredible Face!

Han shouted, when the dust had settled and the other flute-playing Han's face finally appeared over the broken hilltop, lit up like a satellite in the neon-pink dusk. Han ran up the hill in a childish burst of exuberance and, without really thinking, snatched the flute from Han's lips and threw it skyward. It sailed and sailed until it hit a cloud, shattering, all crystalline student symphonic, before raining back down to Earth like the revelatory crumb of an overbaked potato.

Even the crumbs revealed that it had been rotten.

Han's nose started to drip a ghoulish lemon-lime slime and a minute later, the other Han's started to drip too.

"You seem so familiar to me," Han said, wiping. "And yet, I don't believe we've met?"

The twins instinctively pressed their palms together as the wind system in the Northern Hemisphere reversed clockwise and the wind system in the Southern Hemisphere swept the opposite way.

Tiny tornadoes accumulated around their bodies, whistling across their nostrils and activating the melodic threads of their clothing.

Han smiled and the other Han smiled back. Breathing into their difference, their sameness. In and out, out and in…

(Could it really be that Han & Han were so clueless as not to recognize their likeness?)

The breath of the world held its breath for their smiling.

The Breath of Han & Han stopped the world—

Their hands, glowing effortlessly now, pulsed gently to the sounds of far-off bells. They were glowing up to their forearms now, their elbows, shoulders. Glowing like conjoined X-ray fish through their bellies, guts, groins.

Their knees locked fatalistically against the slope of the hill.

"Had I only known…" Han started, as the other Han's body lit up like fluorescent lemon-lime Jell-O.

"I never, ever, ever…" the other Han said, glowing back.

Han & Han embraced each other on the exploded hilltop as the glowing orb of them jiggled and squeaked and eventually rose, all giddy and enchanted, from the broken crest of the hill.

### The Orb of Them Was So Beautiful It Hurt!

The orb grew brighter and brighter until it filled the sky and finally reached a point of nonexpansion. It exploded there, sending a planetary _____ upward and downward and side to side, squealing to the splintered _____ of the _____ and sounding every broken _____ to be found there, sending each squealing _____ up into the most exhaustive _____, _____ totally outside of the average person's natural or desired _____, just twinkling and _____, banging and _____, clanging and _____ and _____ right up into the pillowed _____, even breaking the vaporous _____ itself in gruesome half as if the _____ was no more _____ than a clumsy, secondhand _____, and the _____ of some _____'s cumbersome, untuned _____ was cracking open to reveal the ugliest _____ and _____, the ugliest, most honeyed, most forgiving _____ and _____ ...

...until finally, the orb of Han & Han evaporated, leaving no trace of itself behind.[15]

---

15 *squeal, edges, earth, bell, fragment, keys, keys, vocal range, twinkling, banging, clanging, clanging, atmospheres, mass, air, elegant, piano, noise, stranger, piano, hammers, strings, timbres, springs.*

**The Breath of the World**

inhaled, exhaled.

    Then it carried on.
    Just like that.

*(Poof!)*

# NOTES

"A Woman Suffering" was first published in *Echolocation*, with thanks to editor Finlay Pogue. Thank you to Fabiola Carranza and Agustin Velasco for their assistance with the place names.

"Dreaming Against Capitalism" was first commissioned for the group exhibition *The Pandemic is a Portal* at the SFU Audain Gallery, Vancouver, with thanks to curators Karina Irvine, Christopher Lacroix, and cheyanne turions. It borrows quotes from Karl Marx's "Wages of Labor," Eileen Myles's "An American Poem," and George Saunders's 2013 interview with *The New York Times Magazine*. The final scene in the canoe draws inspiration from a section of Thoreau's *Walden*.

The beginnings of "A Journey, Some Riches, Some Castles, Some Garbage" were inspired by Franz Kafka's novel *The Castle* and originally written on invitation of Aryen Hoekstra for the inaugural reading at Franz Kaka gallery in Toronto.

## JACQUELYN ZONG-LI ROSS

Early versions of both "A Brief History of Feeling" and "Twelve Forecasts" were originally published in *BOMB*. The line about the Pink Panther in "Twelve Forecasts" is quoted from Gilles Deleuze and Félix Guattari's *A Thousand Plateaus: Capitalism and Schizophrenia*.

"Autobiography of a Lover" was originally written for *the ee!* as a response to Mira Dayal's artist book *Hair Biography*. Thanks to the artist and to editors Marci Green and Jason Lipeles for the invitation.

"Elementary Brioche" was only ever completed thanks to the kind encouragement of Sheung-King, who invited me to submit a piece to his guest-edited issue of *The Ex-Puritan*. The chapter titles and grammatical sections are borrowed, reimagined, and/or (mis)translated from the chapter lessons found in a set of Chinese language textbooks entitled *Hanyu Jiaocheng*, third edition, books 1A and 1B. Thanks to my classmates at Shanghai Jiao Tong University for the friendships and adventures.

"Brain, No Brain" is in part inspired by Susan Sontag's journal entry dated December 3, 1961, from *Reborn: Journals and Notebooks, 1947–1963*, which reads: "The writer must be four people: 1. The nut, the obsédé / 2. The moron / 3. The stylist / 4. The critic. / 1 supplies the material; 2 lets it come out; 3 is taste; 4 is intelligence. A great writer has all 4—but you can still be a good writer with only 1 and 2; they're most important." The quoted text by Maurice Merleau-Ponty is taken from *Phenomenology of Perception*. The research on snails is drawn liberally from a variety of popular news articles from 2016 citing recent scientific findings on the topic published in the journal *Nature Communications* (Michael Crossley, Kevin Staras, and György Kemenes's "A two-neuron system for adaptive goal-directed decision-making in *Lymnaea*"), as well as from an article by Joseph Deitch published in *The New York Times* on March 25, 1984, entitled, "Researchers Use Snails to Pursue Secrets of the Brain."

"The Breath of Han & Han" borrows an excerpt from the Wikipedia page on wind instruments.

The title "The Longest Way to Eat a Melon" was loosely inspired by a quote from Lu Xun's 1936 essay "This Too Is Life" in which he writes, "If we ate and drank with long faces all the time, very soon we should have no appetite at all, and then what would become of our resistance? Still there are men who will talk in this strange way, who will not even let you eat a melon normally."

**ACKNOWLEDGMENTS**

Thank you to the artists, writers, editors, curators, and organizers of the many publications, gallery spaces, and artists' projects that continue to make such generous occasions for me and my writing to exist in the world and therein be enriched by others. I am enlivened by your spirit and commitment to community.

Thank you to the close readers and mentors that offered feedback and encouragement at critical junctures in this book's development: Jess Arndt, Catherine Bush, Lucy Corin, Kyo Maclear, Michael Turner. This project would not have been realized without your support.

Thank you to the friends I continue to write for and alongside, and with whom my writing is always in conversation: Darby Minott Bradford, Jac Renée Bruneau, Fabiola Carranza, Aryen Hoekstra, Karina Irvine, Robyn Jacob, Adnan Khan, Matea Kulić, Tiziana La Melia, Katie Lyle, Ella Dawn McGeough, Lindsay K. Miles, Colin Miner, Meredith Preuss, Sheung-King, Yi Xin Tong, Casey Wei.

Thank you to my editor Katherine Webb for seeing the stakes of these fictions I've been holding in my head, and to Jordan Koluch and Joseph Young for the copyedits and proofreading. Thank you to my agent, Kelvin Kong, and to Kristin Renee Miller, Danika Isdahl, Erin Dorney, Joanna Englert, and everyone at Sarabande Books for seeing the potential in this manuscript and rallying behind it to make it real. Thank you to Emily Mahon for manifesting the perfect cover.

To my friends and family for their eternal love and support. For caring for me—for all of us—without limits or hesitation.

To Andrew and Oona for keeping me company even when it meant letting me be, for many, many hours, apart. For a love shown quietly through the permission to live with tenacity, autonomy, and imagination a life in art.

This work of writing is not for the faint of heart. This book is dedicated to all the writers' writers who know why they are writing but realize it in their own time.

Author Photo Credit © Maegan Hill-Carroll

**Jacquelyn Zong-Li Ross** is a writer and editor based in Vancouver, the unceded territories of the Musqueam, Squamish, and Tsleil-Waututh nations. Her fiction, poetry, essays, and art criticism have appeared in *BOMB, C Mag, The Ex-Puritan, Fence, Mousse,* and elsewhere. She holds a BFA in Studio Art from Simon Fraser University and an MFA in Creative Writing from the University of Guelph. *The Longest Way to Eat a Melon* is her first book.

Sarabande Books is a nonprofit independent literary press headquartered in Louisville, Kentucky. Established in 1994 to champion poetry, fiction, and essay, we are committed to creating lasting editions that honor exceptional writing. With over two hundred titles in print, we have earned a dedicated readership and a national reputation as a publisher of diverse forms and innovative voices.